7

Ih

any good, but it was in the same category as the others you like. Plus it sounded fun and the author may be related!

Merry Christmas
Sweetheart

Christmas Secrets

Donna Hatch

Works by Donna Hatch

The Rogue Hearts Regency Romance Series:

The Stranger She Married, book 1
The Guise of a Gentleman, book 2
A Perfect Secret, book 3
The Suspect's Daughter, book 4

The Courting Regency Romance Series

Courting the Countess, book 1
Courting the Country Miss, book 2

Songs of the Heart series

Heart Strings, Book 1

Regency Romance Novellas in Anthologies

Timeless Romance, *Winter Collection* "A Winter's
Knight"
Timeless Regency Romance, *Autumn Masquerade*
"Unmasking the Duke"
Timeless Regency Romance, *Summer House Party* "A
Perfect Match"
"The Reluctant Bride,"
Emma's Dilemma,"
"Constant Hearts"
"With Every Heartbeat"

Single Titles Regency Romance Novellas & Short Stories

"The Matchmaking Game,"
"Unmasking the Duke,"
"Constant Hearts,"
"Emma's Dilemma,"
"The Reluctant Bride,"
"Troubled Hearts,"
"When Ship Bells Ring"

Christmas Regency Romances

"Christmas Secrets"
"A Winter's Knight"
"A Christmas Reunion"
"Mistletoe Magic"

Fantasy Novel

"Queen in Exile"

Interior Design by Heather Justesen
Cover design by The Write Designer, Lisa Messagee

ISBN-13: 978-1979375573
ISBN-10: 1979375577

Published by Mirror Press Lake, LLC

Dear Reader,

Sign up for Donna Hatch's newsletter and receive a free e-book! To subscribe and get a free eBook of her full-length Regency Romance novel, The Stranger She Married, download here:

http://donnahatch.com/stranger-she-married-free-download/

Your email will not be shared, and you may unsubscribe at any time.

Reviews are appreciated, but there is no obligation.

If you like this story, please help spread the word and rate or review it on Amazon here: https://www.amazon.com/dp/B076B6Z7GZ

Please also consider reviewing *Christmas Secrets* on Goodreads and other book review sites.

To find out more about this author and her books, visit

Website at www.donnahatch.com

Blog: www.donnahatch.com/blog Connect on Facebook: www.facebook.com/RomanceAuthorDonnaHatch

Follow on Twitter: https://twitter.com/donnahatch

Thank you!

For my wonderful husband,
who gives me gifts of love every day.

Acknowledgements:

Thank you to my friend and traveling partner in England, Janette Rallison, for brainstorming my plot. My thanks also to my wise and encouraging friends and critique partners, Jennifer Griffith and Wanda Luce, for plowing through a horribly messy rough draft and helping shape it into a story. Also, I am extremely grateful to my beta readers and proofreaders, Tracy Astle, Karen Adair, Julie Moody, Charlotte Morgan, Heidi Murphy, Jean Newman, Jasmine Vanderlinden, and Emily White. I cannot thank you enough!

Another big thank you goes to my writer friends and compadres in American Night Writers Association, LDStorymakers, and the Beau Monde Chapter of RWA, who teach and support me more than they realize.

It really does take a village to raise a child...or a book.

Chapter One

England, December 23, 1813

Holly Gray's courage faded with every step she took deeper inside the castle conservatory where, according to Grandfather's stories, a ghost resided. She didn't truly believe in ghosts, but after listening to story after story, and hearing the family members' comments that suggested some truth to the tales, her imagination had awakened.

Of course, she never would have come here if her sister hadn't teased Holly about being too frightened to explore a dark room alone.

No, that wasn't entirely true. The fault lay with Lord Bradbury. When the handsome young lord had asked Holly if she were truly afraid of a silly story, one of the few times he'd actually addressed her, Holly had declared she was in possession of more mettle than that, and marched out of the drawing room to the location where a ghost might or might not reside.

Inside the darkened conservatory, Holly paused. Others had sought ghosts tonight, even Miss Flitter, and none had returned with frightening tales. Holly had nothing to fear. She steadied her frantic breathing. Through the wall of windows, a bright full moon stretched silver fingers across the floor, glimmered off plants and furniture, and cast deep shadows. Every dark recess suggested a hiding place for a spectre.

All Holly's impulses screamed at her to run back to the safety of the drawing room where her family and other guests awaited. But she didn't dare. With her sister's teasing ringing in her ears that Holly never did anything fun or adventurous, as well as Lord Bradbury's coveted show of interest, Holly pushed on.

Five minutes. She had vowed to remain in the unlit conservatory at least five minutes, then return to possibly gain the approval of—or at least another word from—Lord Bradbury, and never do another daring act again.

There! What was that? A faint rustle. Holly paused and held her breath.

"Who's there?" she whispered. Her voice had quite failed her.

No response. Did ghosts speak or did they only moan?

She let out her breath. Silly. There were no ghosts. She had allowed her imagination to run away with her. She raised her chin and wrapped her shawl more tightly around her to ward off the room's chill.

Despite her heart thudding loudly enough for the guests in the drawing room to hear it, she made herself step forward. She moved deeper into the seating area amidst the indoor garden. Passing plants, flowers, small trees, and pieces of furniture too shadowed to identify, she took a seat on what appeared to be a narrow settee in a group of chairs next to the windows. A dark lamp nearby taunted her. According to her brother-in-law's grandfather, the lights must remain unlit or no self-respecting ghost would appear.

When she returned to the others, she do so with a clear conscience that she had obediently remained in the dark room and yet saw no spirit.

After glancing about the room, most of which remained too dark to see beyond patches of moonlight on the floor, she turned to admire the snowy wonderland glittering beneath the cloudless night sky. How lovely.

She drew and released her breath. She had nothing to fear; friends and family remained a short distance away, Christmas Eve traditions would begin on the morrow, she'd made the acquaintance of a handsome lord who her mother hoped she'd marry, and soon she would achieve all expected of her. Perhaps then, she'd receive her parents' approval and true happiness.

"There you are," a low male voice murmured barely above a whisper.

With a squeak, she jumped.

A soft laugh came in reply and that same low voice said, "Forgive me for startling you."

She tried to peer into the face of the dark figure nearby, but the brightness of the moonlight on the snow outside all but blinded her. Which guest had come to the conservatory? She was supposed to remain alone.

A silhouetted male form neared. "You are so lovely."

Was that Lord Bradbury? Did he truly think her lovely? He'd hardly exchanged two words with her since she and her parents arrived this morning. Who else might have come?

The figure sank into the seat next to her. Before Holly said a word, a warm, gentle, ungloved hand touched her cheek. She froze. A pair of lips pressed against hers. Soft, tender, invigorating, his kiss immobilized her. His lips moved across hers, testing, offering. He tasted faintly of citrus and cinnamon, exotic, and delicious. The heat of his lips lit an answering warmth inside. Oh heavens, she'd never imagined such a sensation! His lips continued to play with hers while a sweet ache formed. With both hands, he cradled her face, and deepened the kiss. An exquisitely delicious sensation carried her closer to an edge she never knew existed. An untouched place in her heart awoke and sang while the hot and cold tingles turned into a foreign longing. Every bone, muscle, and sinew in her body turned to liquid more decadent than the chocolate she liked to drink every morning.

She sighed. A soft male moan came in reply. The kiss ended but his soft lips planted tiny kisses along her cheek, her eyelids, her brow. Holly remained motionless, spellbound by the beauty and power of the kiss. His hands withdrew. She kept her eyes closed another heartbeat, unwilling to release the sensations shooting through her. Who had kissed her? And why? Surely it was Lord Bradbury. Why else would he have encouraged her to come seeking a ghost? She opened her eyes.

She sat alone.

One plant moved as if someone had passed by, yet the room remained all as it had been. Holly was forever changed.

Who had kissed her? He had disappeared so quickly. Like a ghost. She gasped and looked around. She had felt hands. Lips. Warmth. No ghost possessed such things.

Did it?

Surely, she had not shared such a moment with a ghost.

Stunned by the surpassing glory of the

unexpected experience, and grappling with possibilities, she traced her lips with her fingers. Who had it been?

A likely possibility shouted that she had been the unwitting recipient of a kiss intended for another. Heaven forbid! That would be so humiliating—the ultimate form of rejection.

No, surely not. A sensation that glorious could not have been the result of mistaken identity. Likely it had been Lord Bradbury. Her mother would be ecstatic if it were true—not that Holly would tell her, of course. But it did suggest that he admired her more than he let on.

It might also have been a secret admirer who had chosen that moment to make his intentions known, but had decided, for whatever reason, to keep his identity hidden.

The third option was...a ghost? That was mad. He'd felt too real. Too solid.

Yet, could a kiss that magical have been delivered by a mere mortal? She laughed at the thought. It had to have been Lord Bradbury. How mysterious. How wonderful!

"Holly?" Her sister's voice shook her out of her thoughts.

Holly reached for her shawl now laying on the settee around her hips, forgotten in the midst of the mind-numbing kiss.

She might live the whole of her life without a repeat of that extraordinary experience. A sense of loss opened up inside her heart. In the coming years, she would surely revel in the memory of that kiss, knowing that once in her life she had experienced a single, perfect moment. It would remain hers alone, private, untainted by others' approval or disapproval.

"Holly? Are you here?" her sister's voice shook her from her musings.

"I'm here," Holly croaked.

"Well, you've certainly proved your point." Ivy laughed softly. "You only had to stay here for five minutes and you've been here for over a quarter of an hour."

Holly wrapped her shawl around her shoulders, though her skin remained unnaturally hot. "Just ensuring I exceeded my required stay." Holly pressed her hands to her feverish cheeks.

A branch moved, the same branch that had shifted when the man—ghost?—had left her, and her sister's familiar silhouette stepped out. Moonlight shimmered on her silk evening gown and pale hair, the same color as Holly's, thanks to Mama's insistence that she rinse her hair with lemon juice so as to remain fashionably blonde.

"We were concerned about you being here alone

so long," Ivy said. "Are you well?

"Quite well," Holly said with a calmness that surprised her. She left the conservatory with her sister. At the doorway, she cast a glance back, half hoping to see the figure of a man. Disappointment should not have tasted so bitter.

She would never look at this room the same.

Had she been alone? Perhaps it had not been Lord Bradbury, after all.

"Well?" Ivy demanded, with laughter in her voice. "Did you see a ghost?"

How to answer that question? Holly paused. "Did you see anyone else in here?"

"No. Why?"

"No reason. Just wondered if perhaps you saw the ghost instead." Or the man who'd kissed her and left without revealing his identity.

They entered the drawing room lit by candles and a roaring fire in the hearths at each end. Laughter and warmth greeted her. As she and her sister approached, the gentlemen all stood except the aged story teller, Lord de Cadeau, who could not stand without help. Had someone in this room crept out, kissed her, and returned with no one else the wiser?

"Any ghost sightings this eve in the conservatory, Miss Gray?" The eighty-year old patriarch and Ivy's grandfather-by-marriage fingered his cane.

Ivy chuckled. "Of course not, Grandfather. She would have let out a shriek and come running back to us."

Laughter came in reply. Ivy's scoffing, plus the guests' laughter raised Holly's ire. She wrapped her shawl more tightly around her. "I am not so easily frightened as all that."

"Well, then what happened?" said Lord de Cadeau.

"Grandfather," Ivy's husband, Joseph Chestnut, said in gently humorous rebuke. "Perhaps she does not wish to discuss it."

"Holly?" her mother asked. "You do seem flushed. Did you see something?"

"Not...exactly," Holly confessed.

The room fell silent as all eyes trained on her.

"Well, girl, out with it," commanded Lord de Cadeau. "What did you see?"

Holly let out a tiny laugh and tried to wave it off. "I didn't *see* anything, exactly."

Ivy's face took on a triumphant expression. "I knew it."

Holly forged on. "But I did *feel* a..." She let out her breath. How to describe it without telling them she kissed a stranger who may or may not have been a physical being? Surely they'd think her mad. Or fast. Which would be worse? She finally finished with, "A

9

presence."

The fire popped, the only sound in the room. Ivy's mouth hung open.

"What did you feel, girl?" Lord de Cadeau asked with an encouraging smile that revealed a remarkable number of his teeth considering his age.

"Well, my lord—"

"I asked you to call me Grandfather, if you will recall."

She huffed a tiny, nervous laugh. How odd to address a gentleman of his age not directly related to her in such a familiar manner. Surely only as the sister-in-law of the viscount's grandson, Holly ought not to be so informal. Still, one did not refuse such a request from a nobleman.

"Grandfather," she amended. "It was more of a...sensation that someone—some presence—was there." She finished weakly, glancing about the room, half expecting them all to see the truth written all over her face.

The sophisticated Lord Bradbury sipped his drink, his eyes crinkling in amusement as he cast a glance around the room. Dark-haired and grey-eyed, he had the patrician features of a king from a bygone era. He sat back in the armchair with all the confidence of a monarch surveying his domain. From the moment she'd met him this afternoon, Holly had been taken with his handsome elegance as much as her mother had been taken with his title and wealth. Had he been taken enough with Holly to kiss her?

Such an act did not fit his reputation.

"Were you frightened?" Joseph's friend, the vicar asked.

Despite his gentle voice, the vicar, Mr. Berry, watched her with intensity in his eyes. As a man of the church, he no doubt suspected evil spirits were to blame and already planned to have the castle—and her—exorcized. The handsome young vicar had struck her kind and merry when she'd met him. Now, with the firelight dancing in his sandy brown hair, and a focused expression, Mr. Berry seemed alluringly dark and mysterious, like the kind of dangerous rouges Mama warned her to avoid.

That was silly, of course. A vicar would be more trustworthy than anyone. He certainly would never go about stealing kisses.

Who had done it? And more importantly, why?

Though Holly longed to pace as she sorted through possible answers to give in response to the vicar's question, she sank into an armchair so the gentlemen could be seated. "No, oddly enough, I was not afraid in the least. He—or whatever it was—" she laughed weakly, "did not seem dangerous. I actually felt safe." More than safe. She barely managed not to

11

sigh.

Still standing by the hearth, Mr. Berry took off his spectacles and polished them with a handkerchief. Without his spectacles, the angles of his handsome face became even more apparent. Though vicars generally made a modest living, his clothing epitomized the latest fashion—tasteful, understated, and of high quality. Apparently, he had cast off his traditional cassock during his stay with the Chestnuts. Mr. Berry's dark tailcoat accentuated his trim waist and well-formed shoulders. Tonight, his virility seemed at odds with her perception of a vicar, especially compared to the one who served in her parish. It seemed unfair for such a fine face and form to stand at a pulpit delivering sermons on sin and expect young ladies to keep their thoughts entirely chaste.

The pretty young Miss Phoebe Flitter clearly had fallen under his spell, based on the amount of time the couple spent together over the past few days, and he seemed equally devoted to her. Holly almost envied the girl.

Ivy's voice caught Holly's attention. "A presence, you say. How very strange."

Holly refused to look at her sister for fear she would somehow guess the truth behind Holly's experience.

Mr. Berry replaced his spectacles and glanced at

the door. "Where is Miss Flitter, I wonder?"

Holly looked around. The young lady in question had gone to explore another rumored ghost elsewhere before Holly had left on her own quest. Could the poor girl have gotten lost?

Ivy's husband Joseph said, "I wouldn't worry about Phoebe. My cousin knows her way around the castle. Of course, if the ghosts truly are out tonight...." He raised his brows dramatically.

"Surely you don't all believe these ghost stories?" Lord Bradbury said.

Joseph drew his brows together thoughtfully. "I have seen many strange things, heard unexplained sounds. But ghosts?" He shrugged.

Grandfather's mouth pulled into a knowing smile. "Most stories have an element of truth. These tales have been handed down through the generations. I, myself, have seen unexplained sights in most of these rooms—always on moonlit winter's nights. Do not be too quick to judge that which you do not understand."

Young Rudolph Flitter grinned at their host's grandfather. In a few more years and with a foot of growth, the lanky boy would probably cut a dash through town "Any other ghost stories, Grandfather?"

"Well, yes, as a matter of fact, there's one who haunts the castle ballroom. It seems that about two hundred years ago...."

The ancient viscount's voice wove another spell around the group, but Holly remained untouched. One simple truth remained: someone had kissed her.

She would not rest until she had done everything in her power to discover his identity.

Chapter Two

As he polished his spectacles, Will Berry covertly eyed the fair Miss Gray. Her flushed cheeks and swollen lips left no doubt in his mind whom he had accidentally kissed. Not that he'd had much doubt. Even before he had opened his eyes after sharing that transcendent moment, he'd already suspected he'd kissed the wrong girl. Either that, or Phoebe Flitter had dramatically changed. Their previous kiss had not been so...shattering. In fact, it had created little beyond a vaguely pleasant sensation similar to when, at the age of fourteen, he had kissed a pretty and willing parlor maid under the mistletoe. Shouldn't one be more moved kissing a girl he courted?

Kissing Miss Gray. Egads! That was a sublime experience like none other. Nothing that beautiful should have come from a mistake. Still, he should have been more careful to ascertain her identity. He'd mistreated a gently-bred, innocent young lady who'd clearly never been kissed.

Miss Gray put a hand to her cheeks and sighed. Will almost sighed as well. Beneath Miss Gray's serene and proper exterior, lived a woman of surprising passion. The power of her kiss had heated his blood to dangerous levels, but the shock of discovering he had, indeed, gotten the wrong girl, turned him cold. Such a reckless act belonged in his callow youth, not in his new role as vicar. Being on holiday from his parish did not excuse bad behavior.

Before accepting his new position, he'd promised his father to be an asset to the family by conforming to society's expectations of what a vicar should be, and do his upmost to serve in that capacity honorably, never mind that it hadn't been his profession of choice. Every third son in the Berry family served in the church, just as every second son served in the military and every heir inherited the estate. Tradition and honor were firm taskmasters.

Will had given his word to fulfill his duty, and no proper clergymen went about kissing innocent girls without their permission, especially not in dark rooms. Of course, the honorable thing would have been to explain, apologize, and stand still while she delivered a deserved slap. Instead, he'd panicked and fled like a cad, leaving her to wonder who had kissed her, and for what purpose.

Why hadn't Phoebe Flitter been there as planned? As Joseph's cousin, she had visited enough over the years that she could not have gotten lost.

How would he ever explain to her what he'd

done? If Joseph Chestnut learned of Will's transgression, of the way he'd wronged both young ladies, would that strain their friendship? Joseph might feel protective of his cousin, Miss Flitter, as well as his sister-in-law, Miss Gray. He would be horrified Will had done something so foolish, so careless.

Joseph's grandfather, Lord de Cadeau, wrapped up his story. "So, on a winter's eve, when the moon slides through a cloudless night, the ballroom ghost can sometimes still be seen waiting for her last dance."

Phoebe's brother, Rudolph, leaped awkwardly to his feet. Poor lad hadn't grown into his legs yet. "I'm going to check the ballroom to see if there is a ghost." His eyes glittered.

As Will opened his mouth to suggest they instead search for the missing Phoebe Flitter, she returned. Phoebe sank into the spot on the settee her brother had vacated, and adjusted her gloves.

Phoebe Flitter and Holly Gray, in the full light of the drawing room, bore little resemblance. Phoebe's blond hair had more red, her complexion seemed almost ruddy in its healthful vigor, her figure as robust and shapely as a subject in a painting from by-gone eras. Holly Gray's blond hair had silvery tones in it, her complexion a flawless, creamy white, and her figure as slender and graceful as the fashion plates his sisters attempted to emulate.

How could he have confused the two girls? The near darkness of the conservatory could only be partially blamed for his mistake. A lion's share of the blame lay squarely upon his own stupidity. He should have made certain before he had made his advances. His father's words scolding him for his carelessness rang in his ears.

Will focused on Phoebe. "Did you see a ghost, Miss Flitter?" he asked, careful to use her surname instead of her given Christian name in the presence of others. They had not, after all, publicized, nor even formalized, any kind of understanding.

"Oh, no." Phoebe giggled. "No ghosts in the gallery."

The gallery. Why had she gone there when she agreed to meet him in the conservatory? He'd made that clear, hadn't he?

Snippets of conversations between smaller groups drifted to Will, but he focused on Phoebe. What would he say to her? And why had she gone to the gallery? He should have known better than to arrange a meeting place to kiss her. His impulses always seemed to get him into trouble. Just because he outwardly appeared a respectable vicar didn't mean he'd suddenly become a saint. He tried, he really did, but his rash impulses never seemed to quite leave him. They stepped back, sometimes for months at a time, only to resurface. Perhaps he hadn't changed as much as he'd hoped.

He took another sip of wassail and found his gaze returning once again to Miss Gray. He'd never noticed how lovely she was. Her quiet beauty, and that dreamy expression she presently wore, lent her an almost ethereal glow. She hugged her shawl and stared into the fire with a secretive smile playing on her lush mouth. Did he dare flatter himself that his kiss caused that faraway look in her eyes? The Will Berry of his sordid past nodded in satisfaction that his skill had brought her pleasure, but the Will Berry who served as a vicar when he wasn't on holiday, cringed that he'd tainted a pure young lady by introducing her prematurely to some of the pleasures of the flesh. Only a fortnight ago, he'd cautioned against that very thing in a sermon. He really ought to take his own advice.

Phoebe's younger brother returned the prescribed five minutes later, equal parts smug and disappointed, and plopped down in a chair where he slouched. "I told you there weren't any ghosts."

Lord de Cadeau pointed his walking stick at young Rudolph. "Just because you didn't see the ghost tonight, doesn't mean one isn't here."

The youth said mulishly, "You said we could see ghosts on nights like tonight."

"I said you're more likely to see them on moonlight winter nights such as this, not that you would for certain." Lord de Cadeau cast a satisfied glance about the room.

Rudolph slouched in his seat. "There probably aren't any ghosts here at all," he muttered.

Mrs. Flitter, Phoebe's mother, addressed the aged storyteller, "Well, Lord de Cadeau, if you've finished with your scary ghost stories, I believe we ought to retire to our beds. The hour has grown rather late. Good night, all."

After putting down his newspaper, Mr. Flitter, along with the other gentlemen, stood. A chorus of goodnights rang out. Once again, Will glanced at his unsuspecting kissing companion, Miss Holly Gray. Embarrassment, mingled with returning desire, flashed through him.

He'd behaved abominably. That she didn't seem overset was beside the point. He must make restitution somehow. But he was at a loss as to what to do about it now.

Phoebe arose, eyes lowered, and followed her parents out. If he were to go through with his plan to propose to her, he'd best keep his mind on her and not the lovely lady he had accidentally kissed. And who had responded with such unpracticed delight and passion.

Ahem.

Will set down his glass and offered Phoebe an arm. "If I may, Miss Flitter?"

Phoebe hesitated and glanced first at him, then her parents. Mr. and Mrs. Flitter had fallen into conversation as they strolled out of the room, paying no head to either of their children.

"If you wish." Phoebe took his arm.

A bland form of acceptance. Until this morning, her encouragement had been much more enthusiastic. "Interesting evening," he said benignly.

"Oh, indeed." An uncharacteristic throaty quality entered her voice.

He took a closer look at her. Did he imagine it or did her cheeks appear overly flushed and her lips swollen? And her hair, he was quite certain not so many curls had lain against the nap of her neck, nor had it appeared so disheveled. A smile played about her mouth. Will wrestled with the correct way to ask her what had happened to her this eve. If he didn't know better, he would bet she'd experienced her own stolen kiss. But she wouldn't do that. Would she?

"You seem particularly pleased about something," he commented as they strolled through the far end of the drawing room to the door.

"It's been an unexpectedly pleasant evening." She kept her head demurely lowered.

"It *has* been unexpected." He eyed her. "I thought you were meeting me in the conservatory."

A puzzled crease puckered her brow. "When?"

"A few moments ago. Remember how we discussed that Grandfather likes to tell ghost stories, including one about the conservatory?"

"What of it?"

"If you'll recall, I suggested we meet there under the pretense of ghost hunting."

"Oh. I didn't remember."

She had agreed to meet him, hadn't she? He was certain of it. Although, after his experience in the conservatory, he was beginning to think he'd never be satisfied kissing anyone other than Miss Gray.

He almost laughed out loud. It must have been the mystery, the heightened senses and stirred imaginations from the ghost stories, the moonlight, and the danger of meeting for a stolen kiss that caused his reaction to Miss Gray. Surely, if he kissed her again, it would be less remarkable.

The one and only time he and Phoebe had shared a kiss, he had not been so moved. However, if he hoped to be a devoted husband upon marriage, he ought to at least give his intended the benefit of the doubt. Perhaps instead of luring her into a secluded area and kissing her to learn where her heart lay, he ought to behave more circumspectly and simply ask her. First, though, they needed to clear up the mistake. Somehow.

Finally, he said, "So you did, indeed, hunt for the ghost in the gallery? I thought that was an excuse to meet me in the conservatory."

"No, I went to the gallery," she said airily.

When she made no further explanation, he asked as casually as he could, "Did anything unexpected happen in the gallery?"

"Oh, no. Nothing unexpected. As I said, I saw no ghost."

"But you saw someone," he pressed.

She shrugged. "Only a footman. He saw me back to the drawing room after I ascertained no ghost haunted the gallery." At the top of the stairs, she curtsied, the picture of purity and manners. "Good night, Mr. Berry." On the threshold of her bedchamber, she cast a flirtatious glance at him over her shoulder.

He frowned. Her smiles used to be so beguiling. Now? He shook his head. And why was she suddenly calling him Mr. Berry instead of Will? He brushed away his suspicions that she'd been kissing someone else. He was probably imposing his own guilt on her.

"Good night, Miss Flitter."

Holly Gray's kiss, and the way it eclipsed Phoebe's, must be scrambling his good sense. Surely,

Phoebe would learn to be more responsive as she fell in love with him. Such a sweet, pure girl as Joseph's cousin couldn't be expected to kiss like a hoyden. As a vicar, Will needed a good, upright woman who would save him while he attempted to save others— not someone as sinful as himself.

Chapter Three

Holly picked at her breakfast while surveying the occupants of the breakfast room. All night, she had relived her encounter in the conservatory, no closer to discovering the truth. Generally, she had no problem being good, following the rules, doing what was expected. Making good choices brought her satisfaction and peace. But she craved another kiss from the mystery man. Or the mystery ghost. Clearly, she was not quite the good girl she'd always tried to be.

"Holly, dear, are you listening to me?" her mother asked.

Holly started. "Forgive me, Mama. You were saying?"

Mama lowered her voice and glanced at the end of the table where the gentlemen conversed. "I said Lord Bradbury asked about you this morning."

Holly glanced at Lord Bradbury at the far end of the table. His beautifully tailored burgundy tailcoat hugged his shoulders and his crisp white cravat stood out like a patch of snow beneath his handsome face. He was a study in elegance and masculine perfection. "He did?"

"Yes. He said, 'Your daughter has not yet arisen?' See? He has taken notice of you. We still have a fortnight to ensure he considers you as a candidate. By the end of our visit, I am confident he will wish to formally court you."

The handsome lord never glanced her way. Could he have been the one who kissed her? The thought did instill a sense of delight. A handsome figure of a man, with a reputation for being upstanding and honorable, not to mention his status as a peer of the realm, he would make a fine husband. Her parents certainly hoped Holly would turn Lord Bradbury's head or they would not have made the long journey to Ivy's Christmas house party.

Would Lord Bradbury, a man of integrity, steal a kiss without declaring himself? It seemed unlikely, but who else might it have been?

Besides Lord Bradbury, the gentlemen in attendance at the Christmas house party consisted of her father; her brother-in-law, Joseph Chestnut; Joseph's grandfather, the elderly Lord de Cadeau who'd told the stories and invited all the young people to call him 'Grandfather;' the middle-aged Mr. Flitter; and his son the young Rudolph Flitter; and the vicar, Mr. Berry, who was too handsome for a man of the cloth.

Joseph was too loving and devoted to Ivy to do

something so underhanded as kiss another lady. Mr. Flitter's portly build did not match the lean frame of last night's mystery man, thank her lucky stars. This left Lord Bradbury, too honorable to catch a lady unawares; Rudolph Flitter, who was probably all of thirteen and could not have delivered a toe-curling kiss. That left only the handsome vicar, Mr. Berry. A man of the church? Surely not. Ruling out all the guests left the castle servants which seemed even less likely than a ghost.

Mr. Berry stared into his cup of tea, an almost brooding expression marring his striking face. Odd. He hadn't seemed the brooding type yesterday. Perhaps all the talk of ghosts last eve had offended his clergyman's sensibilities.

Which left Holly with no other prospects for who might have kissed her...except the implausibility that the conservatory truly was haunted by a ghost who could take corporeal form long enough to kiss unsuspecting young ladies. It had to have been Lord Bradbury. Still, it seemed so unlike a gentleman of his unimpeachable character.

Mama's voice broke in, "I suggested to Ivy that we have a musical performance later in the week and invite all to participate. You must be sure to perform. I asked Ivy if she knows whether Lord Bradbury prefers harp or pianoforte, but she claimed not to know. You might play both at different times. Although, perhaps you ought to sing a solo as well, at some point. A voice like yours ought to be revealed to its full advantage."

Holly clamped her mouth shut lest she let out a sigh. She genuinely wanted to please her mother, but always being on display, always performing to prove her eligibility as a wife, and thus her worthiness as a daughter, left her fatigued. If she failed to measure up to expectations, she would let down her mother. She would be a failure.

"Don't slouch, dear," her mother admonished.

Holly straightened and glanced down to be sure her morning gown remained free of spots or wrinkles.

Mama nudged Holly and pointed her chin at Lord Bradbury at the other end of the table. As he spoke with Joseph, he accepted another cup of tea and added sugar and lemon.

"You should have tea with lemon." Mama nodded toward Lord Bradbury. "He will like it that you drink the beverage he chooses." She poured Holly a cup and nudged the sugar bowl and a dish of sliced lemons toward her.

Holly made a face. "You know I prefer chocolate over tea."

In *sotto voce*, Mama commanded, "Try it. Tea. With lemon."

Christmas Secrets

Holding back a sigh, Holly accepted a cup of tea and lemon. Then, just to make it more palatable, added a generous spoonful of sugar. Really, she ought to trust her mother's intuition about these things. Her wisdom had helped her brother and sister both find excellent matches with spouses they adored. If drinking tea—with lemon—would help her achieve their goal, she would make the sacrifice. Holly sipped the concoction, careful to keep her expression benign instead of reacting to the taste. Actually, lemon did improve the flavor of tea. She took another sip.

She'd still rather drink chocolate.

And honestly, would Lord Bradbury even notice—or care—what she drank with her breakfast?

As the group finished eating and sat sipping tea or chocolate, Lord Bradbury pushed away his chair and arose to leave the table.

With almost frantic energy, Mama asked Joseph, "What are our morning plans today? Shall we venture out into the great outdoors?"

Holly's brother-in-law drawled, "Today being Christmas Eve, we thought collecting boughs of greenery, possibly a bit of mistletoe, and felling the Yule log a timely activity."

The young vicar spoke, his voice having an oddly warm effect on Holly's skin. "Do you have a lump of coal from last year's Yule log?"

"Of course," Joseph said with a twinkle in his eye. "I know how important it is to you that we use last year's Yule log to light this year's, so we carefully tucked it away for just such a use."

Grinning, Mr. Berry made a magnanimous wave. "My thanks."

Holly addressed the young vicar. "Does your family hold fast to the Old Christmas rituals?"

Rare winter sun shone through the windows and tinted his brown hair with gold as he nodded. "We do. I look forward to our traditions with great anticipation every year. My mother made them feel almost magical." A wistful tone touched his voice. "But my family lives too far away for me to spend Christmas with them now."

"You must miss your family during this time of year, especially," Holly said.

Mr. Berry looked down. Though his lashes concealed his eyes, the set of his mouth betrayed his attempt to hide his emotion. "I do." A long, elegant finger toyed with the corner of his napkin.

Mama stood. "Then it appears we are all for an excursion, then." With a hopeful expression, she glanced around the table and offered a particularly bright smile to Lord Bradbury.

Lord Bradbury inclined his head. "It sounds like a fitting diversion for Christmas Eve."

"In this cold weather?" Phoebe's mother, Mrs. Flitter, glanced outside as if fearing the weather would suddenly burst in through the windows and attack her.

"Oh, come now, Mother," the young Miss Flitter said, tossing her gold curls. "We will bundle up against the cold, won't we, my lord?" She cast a blatantly flirtatious smile at Lord Bradbury.

Holly frowned. Until yesterday, Miss Flitter had shown a clear preference for Mr. Berry, who clearly returned her regard. Now it appeared she had set her cap at the earl instead. How heartless!

Ivy said, "If we are to seek our greenery and Yule log, let us don warmer clothes—hats and greatcoats and the like—and meet in the great hall in a quarter of an hour?"

Murmurs of agreement rang out. The gentlemen got to their feet, and soon all of them had pushed away from the breakfast table. Lord Bradbury strode out first. Mr. Berry moved to Phoebe Flitter and reached for her chair to pull her chair out for her, but she'd already pushed away from the table and leapt to her feet. The vicar checked his step and murmured a greeting as the young lady brushed past him. Frowning, Mr. Berry watched her leave.

Mama shook her head. "Very bad form."

Holly paused. "What is?"

"Miss Flitter. She was openly flirting with Mr. Berry until Lord Bradbury arrived yesterday. Ivy told me they have been courting quite seriously for over a week. Now she appears to have changed the object of her desires. Shameful."

Holly stared at her mother for making such a kind observation. "Poor Mr. Berry. I hope he is not heart broken."

"Miss Flitter probably feels she deserves better than a vicar since her great uncle is Lord de Cadeau," Mama said.

Holly picked up her shawl and wrapped it around her shoulders. "If that were the case, she ought not to have shown a marked preference for him."

"Yes, indeed. It is exceedingly bad form to encourage a gentleman not in possession of all the most desirable traits."

"Mr. Berry seems to have many desirable traits," Holly said defensively.

Mama sniffed. "Yes, he would be a reasonable match for someone like Miss Flitter who is only passably pretty and in possession of an unimpressive dowry. Miss Flitter may not do much better than a lowly vicar, her ties to Lord de Cadeau notwithstanding."

As Mr. Berry left the room, Holly admired his lean, well-built form. There seemed nothing lowly about him or the Byronic beauty of his face, or the intensity in his eyes. Unaccountably, as he passed through the doorway, he glanced at Holly. She blushed at being caught watching him.

"Do his connections and profession really matter all that much?" Her tone came out almost wistful. She blushed again at the silly question.

Mama's voice took on a scolding tone. "Oh, dearest, don't let his handsome face influence you; a vicar is not for you. Lord Bradbury is our goal. My children were not blessed with beauty and talent to settle for anyone less than nobility."

Mama knew what she was doing, and had succeeded with Holly's other two siblings. Her brother, Charles, had married the daughter of a marquis. Her sister, Ivy, married the heir of a viscount who would one day become the new Lord de Cadeau. Joseph and Ivy both seemed happy enough with Mama's carefully chosen selection, as had Charles, with his wife.

"Soon all three of my children will be married to aristocrats." Her mother let out a happy sigh. "My father will be so proud of me and no one in society will dare openly snub me."

The daughter of a wealthy factory owner, Mama had brought a handsome dowry that breathed new life into Papa's ancient family estate. Marrying into the

33

landed gentry had only fed Mama's desire to continue her social climb, and her children remained her only means to do so. If Holly made a match with a mere mister of such humble means, rather than a lord, Mama might never forgive her.

Inside her bedchambers, Holly added a velvet spencer over her muslin gown, heavy woolen stockings over her silk, and stepped into a pair of nankeen half boots. To complete her ensemble, she donned her heaviest cloak. After fastening the frog closures, she pulled on her gloves.

"Ready, dear?" Mama stepped into the room.

"Almost." Holly picked up her bonnet.

"Let us wait another moment or two to be sure you make a grand entrance. Oh, now dear—you will want to wear the blue bonnet—the height in back shows off the thickness of your chignon and the color brings out your eyes."

Holly set down her green bonnet and picked up the one her mother indicated. She held it over the top of her head, close enough for her mother to inspect but not close enough to muss her coiffure.

"And for the finishing touches..." Mama reached up to the side of Holly's head and tugged several curly strands of hair out of Holly's chignon and arranged them around her cheeks. "There. That frames your face so prettily."

"It tickles like that," Holly protested.

"A small price to pay. You are trying to attract a lord. Everything must be perfect."

Why perfection included tickly hairs around one's face, Holly would never understand. Biting back a complaint, she draped her cloak over one arm and held the blue bonnet. Mama glanced at the watch pinned to her bodice, nodded, and ushered her out the bedchamber. With her head high and her posture perfectly straight, Holly glided down the stairs with all the grace her mother had instilled in her over the years.

Lord Bradbury glanced at her, but returned his attention to Joseph with whom he spoke. The vicar, however, met her gaze. Holly inclined her head in greeting and refocused on a point straight ahead. She held her bonnet in one hand at a graceful angle, just as her mother had drilled into her. Again, her gaze strayed to Mr. Berry.

No vicar should be that handsome. His spectacles lent him an air of maturity and wisdom, and the morning light softened that dangerous aura he had radiated last evening. She rather missed it, truth be told.

Near the bottom of the staircase, Holly misstepped. She pitched forward. With a gasp, she grabbed the banister barely fast enough to prevent an undignified sprawl.

"Oh, Holly." Her mother's terse, whispered disapproval for her carelessness penetrated her embarrassment.

Holly steadied herself and sucked in her breath. She ran a hand down her skirts. As the full force of her humiliation hit her, tears pricked her eyes. How could she have been so careless? That clumsy misstep might have destroyed all her chances with Lord Bradbury. Surely a lord needed a graceful wife on his arm for each state and society event he attended. How ever would she manage her bows to the queen if she staggered like a toddler on leading strings? Mama might never forgive her for tarnishing this one chance with Lord Bradbury.

A hand appeared under her elbow, warm and steady. "Did you turn your ankle, Miss Gray?" a male voice asked.

Through her distress, she could not determine the author of that voice. Keeping her gaze lowered lest anyone view her tears, she shook her head, not trusting herself to speak and give away her overset emotions. Such display would only add to her shame.

"Oh, Lord Bradbury," Mama said. "How kind of you to come to our assistance."

Lord Bradbury. Any doubt whether he had witnessed her disgraceful fall now vanished. Keeping her head down until she could rid herself of her unwanted tears, Holly managed, "Thank you." It came out a hoarse whisper.

"Can you walk on it?" the lord asked.

With his hand steadying her, she took the last few steps to the ground floor which gave her a moment to pull herself together. "Yes, my lord. No harm done." She found the wherewithal to manage a huff masquerading as a laugh of sorts. "I'm not normally clumsy."

"I would think not."

After banishing the last remnants of her tears by sheer will, she peeked up at him from beneath her lashes, exactly as Mama taught her, and touched her hair as if to assure herself all remained in place. Only then did she realize she'd dropped her bonnet. "Thank you for your aid, my lord." She finished with a demure downward look before peeking at him again.

He inclined his head in a bow, his handsome face all kindness. "I am your servant, Miss Gray."

"Yes, how very kind of you to help her." Mama put an arm around Holly. "Are you certain you are well enough to walk, my dear?"

Holly nodded. "Yes, Mama," she whispered.

The picture of elegance, Lord Bradbury bowed and stepped back. As Holly stared at her feet, still hot-faced with shame, a hand thrust her bonnet into her line of sight. She looked up into a kind pair of eyes.

His eyes twinkling, Mr. Berry offered her bonnet to her. "I believe this would look better with your ensemble than with mine."

Her embarrassment faded and she smiled at his wit. "Thank you." It came out breathlessly.

"My pleasure," the vicar murmured.

She must be losing her mind as well as her poise, for she could have sworn a husky, almost sultry quality had crept into the vicar's voice. It turned her knees to lemon curd.

Joseph addressed the group. "I do believe we have all assembled. Let us depart for the Yule log hunt, shall we?"

"Well done," Mama whispered into Holly's ear. "You played that perfectly. I didn't realize you had it in you."

Holly opened her mouth to explain she really had mis-stepped, but if Mama assumed she'd put on a show to gain attention, there seemed no harm in failing to correct her. Holly perched her bonnet on her head, careful not to disturb the curls Mama had arranged, and tied the ribbons.

Papa came and offered Mama his arm. Joseph and Ivy paired off, while Mr. and Mrs. Flitter joined arms.

"A pity your sister and her family have not yet arrived," Mama said to Joseph.

"It is," Joseph said. "They may have met with bad weather or road conditions."

"Travel is difficult in the winter, doubly so with all their little ones."

Lord Bradbury bowed to Holly. "May I escort you, Miss Gray?"

"Thank you." Holly placed her hand in the crook of Lord Bradbury's arm.

Mr. Berry bowed before Miss Flitter. The girl sent a longing look at Lord Bradbury and turned a glare on Holly before putting her hand on the vicar's extended arm. Oh dear. Poor Mr. Berry. Holly hoped he had not deeply loved the girl who had clearly switched her focus to another.

Mama caught Holly's attention, looked meaningfully at Lord Bradbury, and gave her a triumphant smile and a rare nod of approval. Holly warmed all over. She'd managed to attract the interest of the very desirable Lord Bradbury after all, and would finally make her mother proud.

Chapter Four

Strolling along a path in the crisp, December air, Will slowed his steps to give him better opportunity to converse with the girl he'd been courting all week without being overheard.

He glanced over his shoulder where Phoebe's young brother, Rudolph, trailed behind. "Your brother does not seem pleased to join our little morning excursion," he observed to her.

Phoebe waved her hand. "No, he would rather go ice skating or sledding."

"There aren't enough hills nearby for sledding, but there is a pond not far from here. Perhaps we ought to suggest a skating party."

She shrugged. "If you wish. I don't skate much."

"Have you ever tried it?"

"Yes. I prefer other activities inside a warm room."

"I see." Why this disappointed him, he could not have said. Surely few ladies indulged in such a sport. "Perhaps with the right company, it will become more enjoyable," he suggested.

Phoebe shrugged again. It seemed her favorite

gesture. "It doesn't usually get cold enough where I live for that, anyway."

What a pity. However, this year had already been colder than usual, allowing Will several opportunities to skate in his parish. It seemed if he did, indeed, marry Phoebe Flitter, he must enjoy that pastime alone rather than with feminine company.

Did Miss Holly Gray skate? He watched her as she moved with all the grace of a swan on a still lake as she strolled next to Lord Bradbury near the front of their procession. Her demurely lowered head made it impossible for Will to see anything of her face, only the thick coil of fair hair at the nape of her neck. No, she probably did not ice skate; she always seemed to behave in the most lady-like manner—except when he had kissed her. He smirked. She should have pulled away, gasped, slapped him...anything but respond with such innocent hunger. Beneath that perfect exterior who lived to please her mother lay a hidden young woman of startling passion.

Odd that Phoebe, who seemed more vivacious in both behavior and appearance, kissed with no true passion, yet the primly perfect Miss Holly Gray kissed with shameless gusto. She certainly was a beauty, too. But her parents desired Lord Bradbury for her, and the lord seemed to take note of her. Besides, Will had already begun courting Phoebe Flitter.

"I hope we go back inside soon," Phoebe complained. "Walking out in the cold is not my idea of a diverting morning." She cast a mulish look at her parents near the front of the group.

Out of duty, Will said, "If you'd prefer, I am happy to escort you inside."

She sighed. "I promised my father I would remain with the group."

"I enjoy the traditions of cutting greenery and the Yule log," Will said. "I hope you will as well, today."

She made no comment. Memories overcame him of tromping through the woods near his home, selecting a suitable log, and sitting astride it like a hobby horse with his sisters while his father and older brothers pulled it home to burn in the Christmas fire. When he'd accepted the position so far from home, he'd never suspected how homesick he would get every Christmas. Perhaps when he married, the pain of separation would diminish as he and his bride observed Christmas traditions and perhaps created a few of their own.

They passed frozen gardens and followed a path as it wound past icy hedges, stone benches, fountains, fanciful statues, and an eccentric folly. After a time, they left the estate land and reached a wide field. An ice-edged stream gurgled past them, leading to the very pond of which Will had spoken. Ice skaters skimmed along the pond's silvery surface, some tentative with outstretched arms, others with the confidence of experts.

"Oh, look." Miss Gray's voice floated above the group's chatter. "The pond is frozen enough for skating." Her cultured tones had undercurrents of delight.

"Do you enjoy ice skating, Miss Gray?" Lord Bradbury asked.

"I adore it."

Her mother, walking just ahead, turned her head and frowned.

Miss Gray quickly amended, "That is, I did as a child."

Ah, just as Will suspected. Miss Gray enjoyed one of his favorite pastimes, but in her desire to please her mother, had cast it aside to be a lady her mother believed would win a lord.

"I enjoy it as well whenever the lake freezes," Lord Bradbury said.

"Did you bring your ice skates, Bradbury?" Will called up to him.

Bradbury spoke over his shoulder, "No, I am afraid I did not."

"Pity," Will said. "I'd wager young Rudolph would like to skate."

Joseph turned around and walked backwards,

still holding Ivy's hand. "We have three or four pairs in the castle, if you want to use them. We could make a group of it."

Miss Gray's face lit up, but she quickly masked it. Instead, she glanced up at Bradbury from beneath her lashes. "It sounds like a diverting afternoon." Did Will imagine a wistful note edging into her perfectly cultured alto voice?

Bradbury inclined his head. "It does."

"Skating?" Rudolph's voice carried to them from the rear of the group. "I would like to do *that*."

"Then we shall," Joseph said.

"Have you always enjoyed skating, my lord?" Miss Gray asked Lord Bradbury.

Will blocked out the conversation between Miss Gray and Bradbury, and turned his focus to Phoebe Flitter. "What Christmas traditions do you enjoy, Miss Flitter?"

"Usually we visit my mother's parents, but this year my mother wasn't feeling up to traveling that far, so we came here instead."

"I am gratified your family traveled the shorter distance required to spend Christmas with all of us."

Phoebe shrugged. "I don't enjoy travel anyway, especially not when it's so cold. A shorter trip suited me."

Will expected her to say something about being

glad she had come because it meant meeting him. Perhaps she wasn't glad after all. Her behavior had certainly cooled in the last day or two. Still, they had seemed well suited. He refused to give up so easily.

"Are you disappointed not to be spending Christmas with your mother's family?" Will asked.

"I think all the fuss is silly. I'd rather attend a ball and meet new people and dance than remain home with all those tired traditions and no one but family."

Her comment set him aback. Since his early childhood, returning home from school to the warmth of family, his mother's joy during the season, and all their family traditions had been an event he'd anticipated for weeks. Perhaps Miss Flitter would be willing to adopt his family customs if they married.

"However," she added. "Grandfather's stories are always diverting, and it has been pleasant to meet new people."

Instead of looking at Will, Phoebe glanced at Lord Bradbury, another friend of Joseph's who had arrived last evening. *New people*. Had she set her sights on Lord Bradbury, too? Will was all too aware that Lord Bradbury possessed a number of traits women considered desirable. Blast the man. And Phoebe had openly eyed the lord a few times. Will had never doubted his own appeal to the fair sex before. Perhaps his discomfort with his new profession had affected his confidence. Surely he'd grow more comfortable with it in time.

"Are you speaking of meeting people such as Lord Bradbury?" Will asked.

She giggled. "He does have much to offer, being a lord and all."

Will ground his teeth. Phoebe Flitter hadn't seemed so shallow until this moment. When he'd arrived to celebrate Christmas with Joseph and his family, and to meet Joseph's cousin, Will had purposely left behind the traditional cassock in favor of conservative gentleman's clothing during his holiday. However, he'd made no secret about his profession. Phoebe had seemed enthusiastic about Will's attentions prior to Bradbury's arrival. Perhaps a girl of sixteen could be forgiven for comparing Will to a titled lord. Most females seemed to have that preference. And Will was not so lily-livered that he backed down from a challenge.

Will turned on his most charming smile. "Then you must be looking forward to this evening's Christmas Eve ball."

She brightened with that same energy that had piqued his interest a week ago. "Yes, I can hardly wait. And no more ghost stories, I hope. Although, last evening certainly proved more diverting than I expected."

A mysterious smile teased her mouth, a mouth that had failed to kiss with the same passion as Miss Gray's...who he really ought not to allow to dominate his thoughts. But really, who could blame him for his smug joy that Miss Gray had clearly enjoyed his kiss? He certainly had enjoyed it, which did not bode well for his commitment to Phoebe.

Of course, he could not quite shake the suspicion that Phoebe had enjoyed a romantic encounter of her own. If so, he would cease his attentions at once.

Did that smack of hypocrisy, all things considered?

Scattered nearby, the married couples chatted with each other, their voices subdued but cheery. Rudolph, his hands in his pockets, trudged along as if he'd rather be somewhere else. The path led the group into a nearby wooded area filled with evergreens mingling with the ice-laced bare branches of deciduous trees. The party wove among the trees, pausing at each fallen log to discuss whether it made an appropriate Yule log. None of them seemed quite right, at least not to Will. Mr. Flitter urged them on, but Phoebe and her mother both cast longing glances in the direction of the castle. Apparently, neither had a great love for being out of doors nor for Christmas traditions.

Was Will being unreasonable with his

disappointment that the holidays meant so little to Phoebe?

Finally, Joseph Chestnut laughed and motioned to Will. "Since the Yule log is your specialty, perhaps you ought to select it."

After a grin at his long-time friend, Will excused himself from Phoebe and tromped off their path into the freshly fallen snow not yet stamped down by those at the head of the group. He eyed every log, looking for exactly the right one. There. In the middle of a clearing stood a beautifully symmetrical tree, and at its feet lay the perfect Yule log, an oak about five feet long and nearly half as big in diameter. It even looked relatively dry, probably thanks to the thick branches of the evergreens surrounding it.

"I found it," he called back to the group.

They made their way to him, Joseph carrying an axe. "This one?" He gestured.

"That would make a lovely Yule log," Miss Gray said. Her cheeks bloomed with color from the cold and exercise, making her so lovely that he had to look away lest he start staring.

"What's special about that one?" Phoebe asked. "It's like any number of logs we passed, isn't it?"

Before Will could answer, Joseph waved the axe. "Yes, indeed. This is the one. It's the perfect size, so we don't need to shorten it. It should fit in the drawing room hearth. Barely. And it's dry so it will burn." He clapped Will on the shoulder.

The gentlemen, including Lord Bradbury, tied ropes around the log and began hauling it back toward the castle. Will threw himself into pulling the log with all his might. Joseph and his new bride had been very kind to invite Will to spend the Christmas season with them since his own kin lived too far away now that had had begun serving as vicar. He owed it to them to be as helpful as possible.

Opposite the log from Will, Mr. Gray also pulled hard, matching him pace for pace. The older gentleman glanced at him and lifted a brow in a sort of challenge. Will grinned and bent low, pulling even harder. Again, the older gentleman kept up.

"I don't see why you didn't just bring a horse to pull it," Phoebe said.

"Pulling it back to the castle is part of the reason it's good luck," Will explained.

Phoebe shrugged again. "It seems like a lot of wasted effort."

Her comment took Will aback. Really, the last two days, she had transformed into a completely different person than the charming girl to which Joseph had introduced Will. It appeared they had little in common, after all, and her affection did not seem genuine the way it had appeared the previous week. Had she merely been toying with him?

49

Perhaps he ought not give up so easily. She had caught his eye when he met her, and Will intended to learn more about her before making a decision. If he found she did not suit him, he would search elsewhere, his mother's edict to find a wife soon, notwithstanding.

His gaze strayed to Miss Gray. She smiled at Rudolph and gestured to the log they pulled. "Admit it, you are tempted to hop on and ride the Yule log back to the castle, aren't you?"

Rudolph frowned at her. "I'm not a child."

"As you say." She smothered her smile but her eyes glittered in suppressed amusement.

Rudolph frowned harder, as if trying too hard to prove she'd been wrong about him. He cast a wistful glance back at the log before fixing his focus straight ahead. "I do want to go ice skating, though."

She let out a tiny sigh. "That *would* be diverting." She snapped her mouth closed and cast a guilty glance at her mother. Then, "I hope you have a pleasant time."

How sad that her mother's personal standards of etiquette deprived the young lady of an activity she clearly enjoyed. Will stumbled over a snowy boulder in his path. He removed his gaze from the lady who seemed to occupy his thoughts, and watched his step as he pulled the Yule log.

"Shall we oblige young Rudolph and go skating this afternoon, then, gentlemen?" Lord Bradbury said.

A chorus in the affirmative responded. They stomped through the woods dragging their log, breathless and cold, yet exhilarated with anticipation of the Christmas festivities—at least, Will was exhilarated. Judging by the heavy steps and drooping shoulders, everyone else began tiring. Everyone, that is, except Miss Gray. Her eyes sparkled and her delighted smile epitomized Christmas merriment.

"Cheer up, lads," Will called out. "This Yule log will bring us good fortune in the coming year."

Joseph, bless him, rallied. "We could all use a bit of good fortune."

Perhaps a song would lift everyone's spirits. His mother had often used such a tactic successfully. Will filled his lungs with cold air and sang, "God Rest Ye Merry, Gentlemen."

Joseph joined in immediately. Although the poor man couldn't carry a tune in a bucket, and got half of the words wrong, he sang with gusto. A clear, sweet voice rang out, picking up the melody. Will glanced back. Miss Gray sang with the voice of an angel. Her father, Mr. Gray, belted out a fine, strong bass. The others joined in the song, too. Heads raised and steps lightened as spirits noticeably lifted. Even the Flitters joined in the song.

A flash of green caught Will's attention. From the bare branches of a birch hung a green, tangled mass of waxy green leaves with snowy berries. "Look!" He pointed.

"Ah, yes," Mr. Flitter said. "Mistletoe. In days long past, I stole quite a few kisses beneath such bowers."

Lord Bradbury's normally composed features relaxed as he, too, must be recalling mistletoe kisses. Miss Flitter giggled without shame. Miss Gray blushed and looked away. Did she recall a similar encounter, *sans* a kissing ball?

"I suppose we need to retrieve that mistletoe, then, yes?" Joseph said.

"I'll get it." Will eyed the scene. A fallen tree leaned against the birch, making a perfect bridge leading to the bunch of mistletoe as if placed by grand design.

The reserved Mr. Gray shifted. "Careful, lad."

Will nodded in acknowledgement. With his hands outstretched to steady him like a tightrope walker, Will scaled the fallen log leaning against the birch. After a hearty tug, the bunch broke off into his hand.

"Here's a fine collection of holly." Joseph's young wife, Mrs. Chestnut, indicated a nearby shrub of holly.

"Here is ivy." Miss Gray pointed to a vine intertwined with the trunk. They grinned at each other and they simultaneously sang *The Holly and the Ivy.*

Mr. and Mrs. Gray joined in on the third note, Will only a note behind. Others picked up the tune almost at once. The group sang merrily as they gathered greenery and piled their findings on top of the log. Once finished, the menfolk picked up their ropes to resume their trek back to the castle. Miss Flitter's lack of enthusiasm showed in her posture, her expression, and her voice. Perhaps she cared little for singing. Not everyone had been blessed with a love of music. But she had many other fine qualities. Didn't she? Joseph had certainly spoken well of her when he'd invited Will to come meet her.

When they'd finished *The Holly and the Ivy*, Will sang, "Here We Come—"

"—A-wassailing among the leaves so green..." Again, Miss Gray joined in first, glancing at Will with shining eyes.

Her father came in only a note behind. The others picked up the tune more quickly this time. Singing lifted everyone's spirits and they almost danced, smiling and laughing all the way back to the castle. At the bottom of the steps, Will, Joseph, Mr. Gray and Mr. Flitter hoisted the log onto their shoulders to carry through the castle to the drawing room. The ladies flanked them. Still singing, they carried the Yule log in a procession that would have pleased Will's mother and brought it through the drawing room doors.

The elderly viscount sat in a chair with a blanket over his lap next to a darkened fireplace. He sang and clapped his knobby hands in time to the beat.

"Grandfather, we have the Yule log," Joseph called out.

"Ah, good, good. Bring it in and let's get it lit." Lord de Cadeau beamed at his grandson, Joseph, and nodded to someone behind them.

A footman, a tall sturdy lad with a shock of red hair, sprang forward, carrying a piece of coal about the size of a fist, and placed it in the hearth. Will and the others lowered the log to the floor and removed the greenery to be used for decorative boughs.

With a gesture, Will asked, "Who wants to be first to sit upon the Yule log?"

Bewildered expressions from the Gray family met his gaze.

Joseph grinned. "It's supposed to bring good luck," he explained.

"Yes, indeed. Who wants the first honor?" Will said.

Miss Gray tilted her head. "You are surprisingly superstitious for a man of the cloth."

Will laughed. "It's not for superstitions that I enjoy these things; it's family tradition. My mother grew up in Yorkshire and brought her Old Christmas customs with her when she married my father. She always makes holidays memorable."

Miss Gray smiled all the way to her eyes. "She sounds like a true delight."

"She is." Will waved grandly at the log. "If no one objects, I shall go first." He sat on the log, grinned at the company, and sprang off. "I feel fortunate already. Who is next?"

"I am," Joseph said. "It must be good luck. A short time after I sat on a Yule log last year, I met the love of my life." He cast a fond look at his bride.

"It was my good fortune as well," the young Mrs. Chestnut said. The love in her eyes as she exchanged an intimate glance with Joseph sent a pang of longing through Will. Holly Gray also watched her sister with admiration and longing, as if she dreamed of finding the love of her life. Mrs. Gray smiled at the exchange between her daughter and husband, and put a hand on Holly's arm, giving it a maternal pat. Perhaps she wasn't as cold as Will had first supposed.

Joseph sat on the log, followed by his young wife, Ivy. One by one all the others, including Miss Holly Gray, sat on the Yule log, even the boy Rudolph, and finally the elderly viscount, with some assistance from his grandson, Joseph, on one side, and Mr. Flitter on the other.

That done, Will and Joseph set the log into the fireplace next to last year's Yule charred remnant. The footman then brought a box filled with dry kindling. A maid brought a bottle of brandy and sweet spices.

"If I may?" Will asked Lord de Cadeau.

The octogenarian gestured. "Of course, young Will, of course."

Lord de Cadeau had been calling him "young Will" for years and probably would all his life. Grinning, Will set all the kindling around the log, mingled with cinnamon sticks and cloves, and then sprinkled the wood with brandy. Using a lit candle, he lit the nearest stick, and stepped back. Flames sprang up. A collective *ahhh* sounded from behind him, accompanied by applause. A Christmas fire. He almost felt at home. Almost.

"What a lovely Christmas fire," Miss Gray said. "It smells heavenly."

"Hear, hear," Lord Bradbury said. "Let us make good use of the heat." He stepped forward, stripped off his gloves, and held his hands out to the blaze, careful not to block it from Grandfather.

Mrs. Flitter tucked the blanket around her father again, one of the few tender acts Will had seen the woman perform. Phoebe Flitter rushed to the hearth, positioning herself next to Lord Bradbury. She clearly gave no thought of the aged viscount behind her, and stood directly in front of him.

Will shook his head and huffed a disbelieving laugh. Had Phoebe always been that thoughtless or had she grown so chilled from their excursion that she acted out of character?

"That does feel good," Phoebe gushed. "Goodness, it was cold out there, wasn't it, my lord?" She gave Bradbury the same beguiling smile she used to give Will.

Her flightiness grated on Will. He'd never been one to fight for the attentions for a girl. Usually females came to him aplenty. Did he want her badly enough to persist? His competitive nature cooled in the face of her true character.

The housekeeper arrived with a pot of tea and one of chocolate. Cups passed around. Lord Bradbury added lemon to his tea and sipped it. Holly Gray indicated she desired the pot of chocolate but after a sharp look from her mother, also requested tea and lemon. Curious.

The group warmed themselves near the crackling blaze. As Will watched her, Miss Gray glanced at Joseph's grandfather.

After a distressed look at Phoebe, who still stood in front of the old man, Miss Gray went to Lord de

Cadeau's side and knelt. "Shall we move your chair closer so you may stay warm, Grandfather?"

Lord de Cadeau patted her hand, paternal affection softening his wizened features. "Don't trouble yourself, sweeting. I have been inside, warm and dry, whilst you young'uns have been out in the cold. Get warm, then come sit by me."

"I am warm." She finished her tea and settled herself on her knees next to his feet.

Miss Gray's mother cleared her throat. "I think perhaps he means for you to take a seat." She gave a meaningful glance at a nearby chair.

Miss Gray flushed and climbed gracefully to her feet. Apparently, ladies vying for a lord's attention did not sit on the floor, according to her mother.

Will sprang forward. "Allow me." He plucked the armchair her mother had indicated and brought it to her, placing it close to the grandfather, but near enough the hearth that she could feel some warmth.

"Why, thank you, Mr. Berry." Phoebe plopped down on the chair and turned her attention back to the fire with an adoring gaze at Lord Bradbury.

Will paused. "Erm, you're welcome. Here, Miss Gray, this one is for you." He brought another chair and placed it on Lord de Cadeau's other side.

Miss Gray smiled as she took the seat. "Thank you, sir, that's very kind of you."

As she sat, a whiff of her perfume reached Will, a blend of vanilla, cinnamon, and orange that combined spring and Christmas in a sweet, warm blend of innocence, cheer, and passion. That scent alone should have been Will's first clue that he'd approached the wrong young lady in the conservatory. Phoebe's unremarkable lavender scent had never called forth tangible images.

Lord de Cadeau addressed Miss Gray. "Here, sweeting, this is big enough for us both." He unfolded the blanket on his lap and spread it over the both of them, the middle hanging limply between their chairs. "Now, tell me about your adventures outdoors."

Will backed up. Clearly, Miss Gray did not need him hovering over her.

Miss Gray launched into a telling of how they found the Yule log, the way Will had scaled the fallen tree like a circus performer to fetch mistletoe, making it far more dramatic and humorous than it had been in reality. She spoke of locating the greenery, what people had said, even going so far as to mimic their speech patterns and accents. Her eyes sparkled and her sweet, musical voice painted images of mirth and adventure. With a touch of longing, she revealed their plans to go skating this afternoon and how she hoped the weather cleared enough for the gentlemen to enjoy their time on the ice.

She really was lovely. Will glanced at Phoebe who had abandoned her chair to engage Lord Bradbury in conversation, her eyes sparkling as she turned her enchanting smiles on him, the kind of smiles she had turned on Will often enough the previous week that he'd thought her affection genuine. Had he been misled about her interest in him? And more importantly, had he been wrong in believing her a good match?

Lord de Cadeau chuckled and patted Miss Gray's hand. "You are a great storyteller, sweeting. I ought to have you tell my ghost stories from now on. People would no doubt prefer to look at your pretty face, anyway."

Holly laughed, not the carefully controlled giggle of a society lady, but with true mirth. "You flatter me, Grandfather. Your stories are vastly diverting. No one could tell them as you do."

Phoebe's laugh, the aforementioned carefully controlled giggle, rang out. "Oh, my lord, you are far too modest." She touched Lord Bradbury on the sleeve.

Lord Bradbury stiffened at her uninvited contact.

Again, Will glanced at both young ladies present. Perhaps he'd been hasty in courting Phoebe. Yet, if he'd raised her expectations, it was his duty, as a gentleman, to offer for her, regardless of his feelings, if she wanted him. It was possible her interest in Bradbury was a passing fancy. She'd seemed so enamored with Will until lately. The fault might lie with him. Had he given her reason to doubt him? She couldn't have known about his mistaken kiss, could she?

"If you will excuse me," Lord Bradbury said. He inclined his head in a bow and strode out of the room. Before he reached the door, he checked his step and went to Holly Gray. "Will you be so kind as to save me a cotillion at this evening's ball?"

Miss Gray smiled graciously. "Of course, my lord. I would be delighted."

He nodded another bow and left the room.

A moment later, Phoebe announced, "I believe I will go change." She gestured to her walking dress where melted snow had darkened the fabric, and shot a cold stare at Miss Gray. Odd, that. Why a sudden disliking for Miss Gray? Jealous of the competition for Lord Bradbury, perhaps?

Phoebe's departure might be Will's best opportunity to have an honest conversation and to determine his next course of action. It seemed Phoebe had set her sights on Lord Bradbury, and Will was disenchanted enough with her to end his courtship. However, he should find out for sure before he stepped back or Phoebe might feel she'd been thrown over. Even in his callow youth, he had not so heartlessly raised a lady's expectations and then cast her off. Although, that course of action appealed to him more and more by the minute.

Will stood. "I shall change, as well." He left the room in Phoebe's wake, and caught up to her in the great hall at the foot of the stairs. Though they were surely out of earshot, he lowered his voice. "Phoebe, since you gave me leave to use your Christian name, and we shared a kiss, I feel I ought to reassure you that my intentions toward you are honorable. If we continue our courtship, I want you to know that I have every intention of offering for your hand."

Startled, she looked up at him. Her eyes narrowed, and a frown tugged at her lips. "Oh."

"Is something amiss?"

"Oh, no, it's only that...well, I am not sure of my heart yet."

"You weren't sure of your heart when you kissed me?"

She pressed a hand to her abdomen and giggled. "It was, after all, only a kiss. Surely you know that just as you have clearly kissed other girls, I have kissed other boys."

Her candor set him aback. True, her kiss had not been unpracticed—simply lacking in true passion. He'd misread her. He finally managed, "I suspected— not that I care to be called a mere 'boy.'"

She giggled again.

He thought back to the previous night. When Phoebe had returned to the group after failing to meet Will, her cheeks had appeared flushed and her hair had seemed a bit disheveled. Will had been so stunned—and guilt-ridden—about his own encounter that he'd dismissed all the signs that she might have had a tryst right beneath Will's nose.

With Will keeping pace, Phoebe climbed the stairs toward the guest wing. "What we shared was pleasant, but you needn't feel obligated to me. I feel no obligation toward you."

He eyed her. "So, you accepted my invitations to dance with me, accompanied me on carriage drives and the sleigh ride last week, choose me to partner you three days ago in whist because...?" he waited for her to provide an explanation.

"Well, I had nothing better to do. And you are the only gentleman here near my age besides my married cousin."

Perfect. She had spent time with him out of boredom, rather than a desire for his company.

Still, he had to be sure. "Why did you kiss me?"

"I enjoy kissing. It's very pleasant, don't you agree? But it isn't a promise or anything." His dismay must have revealed itself on his expression because she added, "Oh, I assure you, that I enjoyed kissing you and I would be very happy to do that again. You certainly do a better job of it than most." She giggled, a sound that once enchanted him but now grated on his nerves, like scraping a fork on a plate too hard. "But I am not looking for a marriage proposal from you. I could never be happy as a vicar's wife."

Her words hit him like a slap. How could he have been so completely wrong about Phoebe Flitter? She was nothing but a shallow, selfish flirt who had discarded Will in favor of a lord. And last night, she'd kissed someone—other than Will or Lord Bradbury. What a conniving little doxy!

"I apologize if I wounded your sensibilities," Phoebe said in a tone that sounded more flippant than truly repentant.

He found a benign tone. "I am relieved to know the direction of your heart, so I may stop trying to convince myself you are a good match because Joseph asked me to consider you and because I took a small liberty with you."

She gave him a startled glance. Yes, such a statement was probably beneath a gentleman but he couldn't help dishing back a taste of her dismissiveness. And besides, it was true. Now that he didn't feel he owed her a proposal, he could look elsewhere for someone who suited him better and behaved more circumspectly. Still, being so casually dismissed by the girl rankled. No girl had ever done so.

Today's events seemed designed to chip away at his pride. Perhaps a vicar ought not to have so much pride, anyway. It served him right for casting off his proper vicar persona and kissing a girl without first learning her heart. For that matter, he probably ought not kiss any more girls until he'd extracted a marriage acceptance. People expected high standards from their local clergy, whether those standards existed in truth.

"Thank you for your honesty." He inclined his head in a vague bow and strode to his bedchamber, equal parts angry at Phoebe for leading him on and angry at himself for not having seen through her games.

He had not loved her. He'd pursued her because she was comely and had seemed demure and came from good family, being related to Joseph and all. His friend had spoken well of her over the years. Phoebe had seemed the kind of girl of whom his mother would have approved—at least, at first.

When Will's mother, as well as the lady of the manor in his new parish, had strongly encouraged Will to find a wife soon, he'd set his mind to the task. A wife would lend him respectability and acceptance that his status as a bachelor could not. However, the parish where he served as vicar had few prospects, thus he'd extended his search farther afield. When Joseph had suggested Will come meet his cousin, it seemed a divine answer. Now, it appeared he must begin his search for a wife anew.

He strode to his room, annoyed with himself for being so thick-headed about Phoebe, and relieved he had discovered her true character before becoming irrevocably entangled with the wrong girl.

Chapter Five

Holly surveyed her reflection to ensure her mother would find nothing displeasing about her appearance. She had accomplished the changing from her walking gown she wore to gather the Yule log and greenery, to an afternoon gown with relatively little fuss, all things considered.

Now warm and dry, Holly turned in front of the mirror and ran a hand down her afternoon gown. The ivory lustring silk gown had a lovely crispness, slimming but with a flowing quality. The long sleeves provided additional warmth from the chill, and the deep green ribbons threaded through the lace at the neck and sleeves matched the ribbon her maid had added to her coiffure. The ribbon would also coordinate nicely with the greenery they would use to make the boughs to decorate the ballroom and church.

Yes, mother should approve. Hopefully, Lord Bradbury would approve as well. At least he'd secured her hand for the cotillion at this evening's ball. Her mother had been in raptures ever since.

Had he kissed her in the conservatory? If not

Lord Bradbury...then the only true contender would be, well, a ghost.

If only she could ask Grandfather about the possibility, but to do so would reveal her part in that scene, and she didn't dare confess to anything so shocking. Or mad. Her lips tingled at the memory and once again, she traced them with her fingers. Would she ever share such a moment again?

Mama stepped through the doorway of her bedchamber, appraising Holly. She frowned instantly. "I instructed you to leave curls at the sides."

Holly moaned. "They tickle me to distraction."

Mama made a sharp gesture to the lady's maid standing by. "Change it and leave curls at the sides from now on, is that clear?"

"Yes, madam." The maid rushed forward.

Resigned, Holly once again sat on the embroidered cushion while the maid restyled her coiffure. Once completed, Holly again subjected herself to her mother's scrutiny.

Mama nodded. "Excellent. If Lord Bradbury fails to take an interest in you, neither your hair nor the gown can be faulted."

Which implied the blame would lay squarely on Holly—her comportment, her wit, her talent. Her grace. The weight of that burden fell on her shoulders like the Yule log the men had hauled to the castle.

"Now, smile," Mama said.

Holly reached into her inner well of fortitude and produced a smile her mother had taught her—one with exactly the right amount of cheer and modesty.

"Well done; that is the right one to give him. Now, let us see if we can't get a stronger reaction from Lord Bradbury. You carried yourself during the walk very well—speaking to everyone equally so as to show no special preference, and even winning the heart of the viscount as you told your amusing tale while we warmed ourselves by the fire. Lord Bradbury glanced at you several times even before he asked you to save him a dance. Miss Flitter's obvious flirting is the perfect foil to your grace and restraint."

A compliment, of sorts. Holly accepted it and tucked it away. No need to confess she had not been playing a part this afternoon, that she'd only been enjoying herself and trying to ensure others did, as well. The desire to please her mother warred with her desire to be sincere. Perhaps her mother's guidance had become instinctive. In that case, was it still genuine?

Holly's turmoil must have shown on her expression, for Mama's softened. She lifted Holly's chin with a gentle hand. "You are so beautiful and you have such grace and pretty manners. You have already won everyone's heart."

Holly swallowed. The compliment should have landed more sweetly on her, but somehow Mama's affection always felt it must be earned.

Mama searched her face, her expression concerned, kind, even. "My dear, you know all this is for you, don't you?"

"Is it?" Holly ventured.

Mama put a hand on each of Holly's arms and gave them a gentle squeeze. "I know I've been hard on you, but I want doors to open to you that I don't have. You deserve to be the toast of the town. As a titled lady, and with your beauty and mannerisms, every member of the *beau monde* will want you at their events."

Holly chewed on that statement. "You must feel very excluded from most of society, don't you?"

Mama dropped her hands. "As the daughter of a cit, I am not welcomed into many circles. More doors opened to me once I married your father, but many still view me as too close to trade to be worthy of notice—especially in London. I don't want that for any of you children. Ivy and Charles are now safe in marriages with titles. We must do the same for you."

Holly nodded. "I understand."

Being rejected simply because a man earned a fortune, instead of being born into one, seemed shallow, but the upper levels of society had their rules and only accepted members of their own. If everyone in Holly's family, including Holly, married well, her mother's social acceptance would also improve.

Papa entered and looked them over. "Lovely, my dears, both. I am a lucky man."

Her mother clucked at him as she and Holly each flanked him. Papa patted Holly's hand as it rested on his and gave her an encouraging smile. All was well. They descended to the main floor. This time, Holly stepped more carefully so as to avoid another embarrassing tumble, although her father's arm lent her a sense of security.

In the ballroom, Holly spotted Mr. Berry, Joseph, and Ivy, among a veritable army of servants assisting with the Christmas decorations for tonight's ball. Ivy looked harried. As the new lady of the home, she'd only hosted one other ball, and seemed overwhelmed by how much remained to be done for the evening's festivities.

"How can I help?" Holly asked.

"You could tie ribbons on the boughs over there when Will finishes assembling them." Ivy pointed to a table where the vicar cut and bound greenery. Will. Probably short for William. William Berry. It sounded like the name of a poet.

"Will?" Holly teased. "Are you on familiar terms with the vicar, then?"

"Well, that's what Joseph always calls him, so I suppose I have grown to think of him that way." She shrugged, then resumed her lady-of-the-house demeanor. "Papa, please help Joseph hang the mistletoe balls over the doorway. Mama, can you direct the servants where to place the candelabras? I fear there will be too many dark shadows."

They scattered to do Ivy's bidding.

At the table laden with boughs, Holly took an empty seat next to Will Berry. "Shall I start with these, then?" She gestured to the boughs already tied with twine.

"Please." The vicar kept his gaze on his work. "They need a bow and then a sprig of holly."

Holly tied a bow around the center of the bough and attached the holly sprig as directed. The bright red ribbons matched the berries. "That's very pretty. So festive."

A twinkly sort of grin brightened his features. "This is how my mother does it. Your sister was kind enough to let me do it this way. These make it feel more like home."

"Family traditions such as these are lovely. Your mother sounds like a delightful lady."

"She is. She makes every event, however small, feel like a celebration." He continued arranging and wrapping and tying, his head bent over his task. His

72

brown hair shone chestnut in the afternoon light. He glanced at Holly. "I thank you for your assistance."

"It is my pleasure."

She fell silent, relaxed in the vicar's comforting, almost familiar, presence. Yet each time he moved, his subtle, masculine scent of bergamot and something she could not name, wafted to her. She inhaled deeply, and her easy comfort took a sudden turn toward a less wholesome sensation, calling up an unbidden memory of a pair of warm lips on hers.

"Miss Gray, may I ask you an impertinent question?"

She started. Had he guessed the direction of her wanton thoughts? She swallowed. "Of course."

"You seem as if you have something troubling you."

"Do I?" she practically squeaked.

"You have been somewhat pensive, cautious even, since last evening. Are you unsettled by that— erm, what did you call it?—'presence' you felt in the conservatory?"

She paused, choosing her words with care, but nothing seemed appropriate. Or true. Finally, she asked, "Are you thinking of having an exorcism?"

He chuckled. "No, not unless you wish it. I merely desire to know if you are uncomfortable about it, by anything that happened, or that you imagine may have happened." He glanced up at her then, curiously intent, and yet kind and concerned. "I would ease your mind, if I could."

She let her hands fall idle. If she were to trust anyone with her secret, surely she could trust a clergyman. "As a matter of fact, something unexpected did happen." She glanced around, but the others were busy. The din of conversation from her family and servants provided the perfect cover for such a sensitive dialogue.

He leaned in slightly. "You may confide in me, Miss Gray. I assure you, I will not tell a soul."

She lifted her brows. "You want me to make a confession?"

He smiled. "If you wish to call it that." How handsome he was when he smiled. "Or a confidence."

A confidence. She rather liked that. The strain of such a secret had become a heavy load to carry alone. Mama would have a fit of apoplexy if she knew. Ivy would laugh and ask for details Holly preferred to keep private. Papa would probably insist on an inquiry. But a vicar, yes, she could tell him.

"When I was in the conservatory," she took a breath. This was more difficult than she'd expected. She dropped her voice, though she had no need. "Someone...kissed me, but I don't know who it was."

He gave her his full attention. "How could you not know?"

74

"I was looking out the widow, and the moon was so bright and full on the snow that it momentarily blinded me. When he—whomever it was—appeared, I could not see who was there, only a silhouette. He sat next to me. Then he kissed me."

Very gently, he asked. "Were you angry? Frightened?"

She huffed a laugh, his compassion and lack of condemnation only fueling her guilt. "I know I should have been, but he was so gentle, and the experience was—forgive me—but so...very *pleasant* that I was neither angry nor frightened. I was quite overcome in the best possible way." She sighed as the sweetness of her experience overtook her. "By the time I opened my eyes, he was gone."

He studied her as if searching for something. To his credit, he did not appear shocked or repulsed, only intensely focused.

She added, "I vow I never saw him, not enough to identify him."

Very softly, he asked, "Who do you think it was?"

"I am at a loss. What little I saw of his form gave me cause to believe that he was lean and tall, but beyond that, I have no idea. My first thought was that for some reason Lord Bradbury had chosen that moment to make his attraction to me known, in a rather unconventional manner. But he seems too honorable to go about stealing kisses, and not so terribly enamored with me. I cannot imagine anyone else in the household would have done it."

"Hmmm. That is a mystery."

"My only other thought is ...well, it's hard to even consider."

"What is it?"

"You might laugh. Or perform that exorcism in truth."

He tilted his head, his eyes wide. She'd never noticed what a beautiful shade of blue they were, like a clear winter sky.

"Exorcism?" he asked. "Do you think a *ghost* might have done this?"

She let out a helpless half-laugh. "Either that, or a servant, which seems preposterous."

He sat back as if pondering, then resumed his task. "That is something to consider. I agree you are right about Lord Bradbury. I do not know him well, but he strikes me as too honorable to engage in that type of behavior."

"That is my opinion as well."

They resumed their bough making and bow-tying in silence. She could not guess his thoughts, but hers returned to that night in the conservatory, the sublime beauty of that particular intimacy.

The vicar's voice broke into her thoughts. "I believe you may be right."

"I'm right?" She blinked.

"It might have been a ghost."

She almost dropped her ribbon. "Do you truly believe that?"

"Let's consider all the other possibilities."

Working side by side, they discussed each male guest, and every servant that they had seen or met in the castle. The vicar, having spent so much time at this castle over the years in his friendship with Joseph, knew all of them. They went back over what few physical attributes she had detected about her mystery man, and compared them to each male in the household. One by one, they eliminated them all.

Finally, the vicar said, "It is possible that your mystery man mistook you for someone else."

She winced. "That would be truly terrible. How humiliating."

He said nothing for a long moment while they worked. Quietly, he asked, "Can you think of anyone we have not yet considered?"

She worked at her bow, trying to get the loops the same size. "No, I can't."

A weighted pause. "Then the only other explanation is that some stranger entered the castle."

She shivered. That thought frightened her more than the others.

While Holly grappled with the prospect, the vicar said what they were both thinking, "Either it was someone else we have not considered, or it was a ghost."

A ghost.

That would explain why the sensation had been so...unearthly.

Perhaps it had been a ghost. That would be good. She no longer had reason to agonize over who it might have been. She had no reason to fear the encounter might one day come to light and tarnish her reputation. More importantly, she could stop feeling guilty for enjoying the pleasure so much.

Sooner or later, she must also accept that the extraordinary experience was not something she would repeat. Ever. A disheartening realization.

Still, in future quiet moments when she needed a reprieve or a bit of joy, the experience would remain hers alone to recall. To cherish. To mourn.

"I've never seen so many emotions cross someone's face in such quick succession," the vicar said gently. "Does my conclusion trouble you?"

"Probably not as much as it should," she confessed.

He refocused on his bough, deftly tying the last one. "Either way, you have no reason to feel any guilt over it. You were clearly blameless."

She leaned in. "Does it change anything if I were to confess that I liked it—very much?"

He studied her, something hidden and almost vulnerable in his eyes. "Did you?"

She could not hold back her guilty smile. "I did."

His mouth lifted at one corner as if hiding a smug smile. Surely, she misread that expression. He probably thought her silly. Or shallow. Or unladylike.

He reached over and started tying ribbons and holly onto the boughs she had not yet completed. "It does not change anything, Miss Gray. It is a perfectly normal response to an act that is meant to be enjoyed, although preferably between people who are better acquainted."

She laughed softly. "I don't suppose I'll have much opportunity to become better acquainted with my ghost."

"Not unless you lurk in the conservatory every night there is a bright moon. Even then, that might have been an isolated incident for reasons you may not have any way of knowing."

She nodded, sobering. "So, am I forgiven?"

He chuckled, "I'm not a Catholic priest and this isn't Confession."

For some reason, she felt the need to add, "It was my first kiss, I vow."

An inscrutable expression passed over his features. He leaned forward and looked her in the eyes. He really was so very handsome. She forgot to breathe.

"I believe you. And there is nothing for which you need feel guilty. The guilt lies squarely on the shoulders of the cad who used you in such an underhanded manner, man or ghost."

She looked down. She hadn't felt as 'used' as she probably ought to. Even now, the memory of that sensation gave her delicious little shivers.

"Are you two finished yet?" Ivy called to them. "We need more for this end of the room."

Mr. Berry stood. "These are ready." He scooped up an armful of boughs all tied with red ribbons and adorned with holly and carried them to Ivy.

Holly continued working on the remaining boughs.

"Pretty."

She looked up to see Lord Bradbury standing opposite her. He'd sought her out. Wouldn't her mother be pleased? "They are, aren't they?"

"May I be of some assistance?"

She smiled. "Thank you. I have only these left to do. You may do some if you wish."

He sat in the chair Mr. Berry had vacated. "I'm not certain I've ever attempted to do this sort of thing."

"Does your family have any traditions for the Christmas season?"

"My mother thinks Christmas is for attending

church, and that any other type of celebrating smacks of heathenism."

Oh my. That sounded bleak. "Does your father agree?"

"He died a few days before my birth."

"I'm sorry to hear that."

"Thank you," he replied evenly.

He tied a bow around the nearest cluster of greenery. She glanced at him from underneath her lashes. He was a handsome man, as well. With strong, patrician features, clear, intelligent eyes, and wide shoulders, he would be any girl's dream of the perfect suitor.

Feeling the weight of watching eyes, she glanced at her mother, whose triumphant smile could not have been mistaken. Hopefully, Lord Bradbury remained unaware of her mother's reaction.

Holly focused on the gentleman in question. "If Christmas is not a joyful event for you, why have you come to celebrate Christmas with Joseph and Ivy?"

"Joseph has invited me the last several years. This time I decided to accept."

"What was different about this year?"

"I am trying to make up for missing their wedding."

"A kind gesture, to be sure."

"Do you think I'm forgiven?" Lord Bradbury's mouth took on a faintly wry smile.

She nodded. "Joseph doesn't seem the type to hold a grudge."

"No, he isn't."

"Otherwise, he would be less happy with my sister. Ivy can be trying."

He nodded. "Can't we all?"

She laughed softly. "I suppose so."

Lord Bradbury focused on his ribbon as if it were a fencing opponent that needed to be conquered. After a few attempts, he wrested it into submission and pushed it toward her, tied to perfection, complete with a sprig of holly exactly in the middle. He probably did everything flawlessly.

"Is this acceptable?" he asked.

"It is perfect." She smiled.

Grimly, he attacked another bough and said nothing further.

Holly searched for a way to engage him in further conversation. "Have you known Joseph long, my lord?"

"Only about five years. But he's an easy friend to have."

"Yes, he does seem to be. He makes my sister happy."

They worked silently until they'd completed every bough.

The vicar returned, bringing with him an energy that revitalized Holly. "Oh, you finished. Well done."

Holly scanned the ballroom. "Where shall we put these?"

"This group is for St. Nicholas's church. I am on my way to decorate it next."

"Is there to be a Christmas Eve service tonight?" she asked.

"No, the tradition in this parish is a Christmas Eve ball at the big house." He made a general gesture that encompassed the castle. "The Christmas service is held Christmas Day. Apparently, the local rector likes to decorate but suffers from rheumatism, so I thought to help him put up the greenery today to help get it ready in plenty of time." He piled the boughs in a large wooden box. "Thank you for your help."

Lord Bradbury said, "Shall Miss Gray and I assist you?"

Holly smiled at Lord Bradbury's thoughtfulness and willingness to help. He'd even included her. Did he truly have a preference for her, then? Her mother would be so pleased.

She said to Mr. Berry, "If we both help you, we are sure to finish in time to return for tea."

"Yes, that's it exactly," Lord Bradbury said.

"What are you all talking about?" Miss Flitter asked as she sashayed to Lord Bradbury's side.

Mr. Berry stiffened but said in an even voice, "We are about to assist the local rector."

"Oh. Are you going?" Miss Flitter asked Lord Bradbury with a beguiling smile.

"Yes," He replied. "You probably should—"

Her face brightened. "I'll come help, too."

Oh dear. Miss Flitter's mother really ought to have schooled her in comportment. Holly sometimes bristled against her mother's tutelage, but at least she had learned never to throw herself at a man in such an obvious way.

Smoothly, Mr. Berry said, "I believe the three of us, as well as Miss Gray's mother and the parish rector, can handle the decorations at the church. Mrs. Chestnut, however, is still preparing for the ball. I'm sure she needs you here."

Mama arrived at that moment. "Miss Flitter, your mother wants you."

Miss Flitter's expression fell. She went to her mother who was arranging the centerpiece on the serving table.

Holly said, "Mama, our good vicar here is in need of help decorating St. Nicholas's church for tomorrow's Christmas Day service. Apparently, the rector could use some assistance. Lord Bradbury and I thought to assist him. May I?"

"Oh, how kind, my lord." Mama smiled at Lord Bradbury before answering Holly. "Of course you may go, dear. Ivy is seeing to the last-minute details so I will accompany you as chaperone."

"Excellent," said Lord Bradbury. "Let us be on our way—so we may be back in time for tea. We can take my coach." He made a gesture and ordered his carriage brought around without giving Miss Flitter a second glance.

No doubt Mama was in raptures over this development. Others benefited as well; it would help Lord Bradbury escape Miss Flitter, which served her right for casting off Mr. Berry. But most importantly, they would aid the local rector in readying his church for Christmas Day service.

Spending more time in Mr. Berry's company probably shouldn't create such a thrill, but she couldn't help liking him. He was everything kind, but also pleasant and merry. And she would not be a female if she overlooked his good looks. His good breeding and gentlemanly conduct showed in his every word and deed, with the exception of those rare moments when something almost roguish peeped out, suggesting Mr. Berry had many layers. How intriguing. If only he were higher up on the social ladder than a vicar. If only Mama had not set her heart on Holly marrying a lord, and only a lord.

Chapter Six

Sitting next to Lord Bradbury in the rear-facing seats, and across from Miss Gray and her mother, Will relaxed against the pillow-like seats. The luxurious conveyance, courtesy of Lord Bradbury, all but glided over the frozen road toward St. Nicholas's church. If more snow fell, they'd soon need a sleigh for traveling.

Will glanced at Miss Gray, her eyes alight as she looked out of the windows. She'd proven a delightfully surprising girl. She shifted, and again her fragrance reached him. All the sweet sensations of kissing her returned full force.

It was my first kiss, I vow, she'd said earnestly.

He had opened his mouth to say *I know*, but caught himself just in time. He'd been honest when he'd told her the guilt lay squarely on the shoulders of the cad who used her in such an underhanded manner.

The sad truth glared at him: he wasn't sorry. When she had looked down after admitting she'd enjoyed the kiss, a blush coloring her cheeks, and a smile touching her mouth, it was all he could do not to smirk. Really, he ought not be so pleased that his ungentlemanly—his un-vicar-ly—conduct brought her such enjoyment. It had certainly given him a great deal of pleasure, which only proved him a hopeless pretender. A fraud.

He sighed and adjusted his spectacles. He had hoped the eyewear would help him behave in a more circumspect manner. Scholars often wore spectacles, and no rakes of his acquaintance did, so he'd acquired a pair to help him behave more appropriately. Apparently, it took more than a bit of bent wire and glass to transform a sinner into a saint.

"Do you decorate your parish church, too, Mr. Berry?" Miss Gray asked, her blue eyes fixing on him.

"I only took the position last January so I am not yet aware of the local customs. When Joseph invited me to visit him, I found a temporary replacement in the form of a traveling rector. I suppose I ought to inquire about the previous vicar's customs so I don't upset anyone with my radical new ideas." He grinned.

"My parish church decorates for Christmas with only candles and a bit of greenery," Lord Bradbury said. "It's the one festive sign my mother believes is appropriate."

"Is she so very pious, then?" Miss Gray asked.

"Very." A weight settled on Bradbury's words, piquing Will's curiosity, despite his disliking for the lord who was the object of every female.

Mrs. Gray said with the correct amount of respect and admiration, "She must be very proud of you, my lord."

Bradbury merely said, "Perhaps."

Will ought to like the man, but the idea that Miss Gray would likely marry him made a strangely hollow place inside Will, and engendered an inexplicable dislike for the lord. Yes, Bradbury probably deserved a sweet young lady like Miss Gray—far more than Will did, for a number of reasons. Perhaps learning how false Phoebe had played him chipped his confidence and left room for a jealousy that had no business being there.

Of course, no matter what, Will had tasted her lips before any other man. Nothing would change that. He tamped down a surprising surge of arrogant possessiveness and idly watched a few snowflakes drift by.

Mrs. Gray, an admittedly attractive older version of her daughter, focused on Lord Bradbury. "Where did you get your education, my lord?"

"Oxford, ma'am."

"Ah, my husband is from a devout Cambridge family, but we won't hold the difference against you." She smiled with a teasing twinkle in her eye.

His attention piqued, Will glanced at Bradbury. "I attended, Oxford, too. Which college?"

"Balliol."

"Ah. Mine was St. Joseph's." Funny how old school rivalries faded after a few years; Will's odd sense of competition for the lord had nothing to do with college.

"I detested Latin," Lord Bradbury said.

"Did you? I suppose since I grew up speaking so many languages that it came second nature."

Bradbury lifted a brow. "What languages?"

With the proper amount of nonchalance, Will said, "My father fancies himself a linguist, so I learned French, Italian, Spanish, and German along with Latin. He always said if the infernal war ever ends, we'd visit all those countries."

"I don't suppose as a vicar you have much opportunity to travel," Mrs. Gray said.

Did she intend to sound so condescending? Perhaps she had not meant it as a reminder of his inferior status, but it irked him still the same. Really, when had he gotten so touchy about everything?

Lord Bradbury said, "I seldom travel either—except when I'm compelled by some sort of duty to which I must attend." He gave Will a conspiratorial glance, suggesting he'd said that to help Will save face.

Will's dislike for him relented a bit. Bradbury wasn't such a bad chap. Will really ought not sulk like a child who didn't get the last piece of candy.

Mrs. Gray resumed her subtle fawning over the lord. "If I recall correctly, your family seat is in the Lakes District, my lord?"

"It is." Bradbury glanced at her and then back out the window.

"Beautiful country," Mrs. Gray said. "We occasionally spend summers in Windermere."

Miss Holly Gray's sweet voice joined the conversation. "It must be difficult to leave behind all that lovely country and travel to London to serve in Parliament."

"It is fine country, indeed," Lord Bradbury said. "But I enjoy the change of pace in London."

They reached St. Nicholas's church. Bradbury's footman opened the door and set out the step. Will held back, allowing the lord to exit first and have the honor of handing down the ladies. They both thanked the lord, Miss Grey with reserved but sincere gratitude, yet Will caught a calculating glint in the mother's eye.

Mrs. Gray addressed Will. "Mr. Berry, please do escort me to the church."

"Of course, Mrs. Gray, I'd be happy to." He held out an arm and led the way.

Behind him, Lord Bradbury spoke to the carriage driver. Will glanced back. The footman picked up the box of greenery and carried it inside. Bradbury bowed to Miss Gray and offered his arm, which had probably been Mrs. Gray's plan all along—practically forcing Lord Bradbury to escort her daughter. Did Lord Bradbury see through her machinations? With such a beautiful and gracious lady on his arm as Miss Gray, did he care?

"Mr. Berry," Mrs. Gray leaned her head toward him and lowered her voice.

Ah. Of course. A second reason for her wishing him to walk with her. He braced himself for her stay-away-from-my-daughter-who-is-destined-to-marry-a-lord speech.

"You seem an honorable man, and as an old friend of Joseph's, you are a welcome guest in my oldest daughter's home."

He almost nodded. Yes, that was the perfect lead up to the looming let down.

"I looked you up in Debrett's," the woman continued. "Your family pedigree certainly places you on the upper rungs of the social ladder. However, you must understand that my daughter has been raised to marry a lord, not a country vicar with a modest income. Officially, we are here at the behest of my daughter Ivy and her husband for Christmas. However, we accepted their invitation only after learning Lord Bradbury would be present; otherwise we would not have made such a long journey through such unseasonably harsh weather conditions."

Her words came as no surprise. But the sensation of having been kicked in the gut did. Odd. Phoebe's dismissal had not left him so winded. Had the unexpected kiss affected his sensibilities? He didn't normally form an attachment for young ladies so soon after meeting them, or even after kissing them, Phoebe being a perfect example.

Mrs. Gray patted his hand with what she probably meant to be maternal affection, but it came out patronizing. "I hope you can appreciate my position; I want more for my daughter than you can offer her—through no fault of your own."

He stiffened. "Madam, I assure you that I have no designs on your daughter." He opened the gate to the church and held it open for her, all the while gritting his teeth.

She beamed as she passed him. "I'm happy to hear that. You seem a respectable gentleman. I'm sure there are plenty of young ladies out there for one such as you—the daughter of a country squire, perhaps—"

He stopped listening to the woman. For the daughter of a man who sullied his hands with trade to be so high in the instep made her the worst sort of snob, not to mention a hypocritical social climber.

Still, she was right. His modest position in society, with a salary to match, didn't exactly make him the year's most sought-after bachelor. Even without her father's noble ties, Miss Gray's beauty and grace and comportment practically demanded a husband in the highest levels of the *ton*. She probably had a dowry that even most lords would find hard to resist. As a youth with no long-term romantic goals, Will's charm and good looks opened any door he wished. Settling on a humble profession and seeking a wife rather than an amusing diversion changed everything.

He opened the church door for her. "Thank you for your counsel, Mrs. Gray. Be assured that I will, of course, respect your wishes."

He stepped into a dim, tiny foyer and entered the nave lit only by filtered light struggling through the stained glass windows along both sides. The rough-hewn beams crossed the high ceiling, dark against whitewashed walls. A nearby font greeted them as if to remind them of their christening when they were babes. A wooden pulpit stood on the left side of the nave.

"What a charming little church," Miss Gray said in reverent tones. "Not having a transept makes it feel humbler somehow—more like a place to worship instead of a place to be awed."

Will shouldn't have been so pleased by her comment. Nor should he have added, "It's much like my parish church, only mine is a little larger and older—it dates from the tenth century."

"How wonderful to serve and worship in such an ancient holy place," Miss Gray said with a glance at Will. She pointed to paintings over the doorway. "Those appear medieval."

Lord Bradbury nodded. "They do. The twelfth century, I should think."

Mrs. Gray, never one for being left out of conversations, chimed in, "Many churches were built over sites once used for pagan rites. I suppose that was the Catholic church's way of encouraging pagans to embrace Christianity. Isn't that right, Mr. Berry?"

"So I understand," Will said.

Miss Gray admired the interior a moment longer, her expression an enchanting mixture of admiration and reverence. Her eyes shone and her genuine smile dazzled him.

"Welcome," a male voice greeted them. An aged man wearing humble clothing approached them. "I'm Mr. Appleby, rector here. Forgive my attire; I leave off my cassock when I perform messier tasks. How may I help you?"

"Good afternoon, sir." Will approached. "I'm Will Berry, a guest of Mr. and Mrs. Chestnut. May I present Lord Bradbury, Mrs. Gray, and Miss Gray?"

After they exchanged greetings, Will continued, "We have come with greenery and an offer to help prepare your church for Christmas services tomorrow."

"Oh, how very kind," Appleby said. "The family up at the castle is so very good to me. I accept your help, gladly. My rheumatism is acting up and I wasn't sure how I'd be able to get the candles up, let alone add any other ornamentation."

"Where would you like them to be placed?" Bradbury gestured to the box of greenery the footman had left in the aisle.

At least the lord was willing to be helpful rather than simply order around an army of servants.

The rector said, "We usually put some in the windowsills. Do you have any better suggestions?"

Mrs. Gray spoke first, "To tell you the truth, Mr. Appleby, I'm surprised you're decorating a church at all." She glanced at Lord Bradbury as if seeking clues from him. When he only watched her with a mild expression, she added, "Although, we trust your judgment. If we are to decorate..." she spun a slow circle to survey the room.

"We could wrap the longer ones around the columns nearest the pulpit," Miss Gray interjected, "and the shorter ones we could set on those ledges, and I do think they would be pretty in the windowsills. Do we have enough greenery for that?" She turned one of those bright smiles on Will. For a moment, he could barely remember his own name. She truly was one of the most beautiful girls he'd ever met.

He nodded. "I think we do. I'll get a ladder. Lord Bradbury, would you care to assist the ladies?"

"Of course." Bradbury picked up a bough of greenery.

There. That ought to satisfy Mrs. Gray that Will would cooperate with her scheme to throw her daughter at Bradbury. If the lord wasn't smart enough to catch her, he was a fool.

Will asked the rector, "Where might I find a ladder, Mr. Appleby?"

The rector gestured, "Follow me, please." He hobbled as he led Will outside and through a sleeping garden. "Where are you from, young man? What did you say your name was?"

"Will Berry. Originally, I'm from Yorkshire, but I recently moved to a little town south of Manchester when I accepted the position of vicar."

"Ah, fellow clergyman. On holiday, are you?"

"Yes, Joseph Chestnut and I are old friends. He guessed, rightly so, that I'd be homesick during the Christmas season and invited me to join him this year. Although, I expect to remain in my parish in the coming years to hold Christmas services."

"That would be a good way to form a connection to your new parish. Are you married?"

"No, I have made that my next goal, and it is another reason I have come to visit Joseph. He wanted me to meet his cousin, but we have not formed an attachment, so I must seek prospects elsewhere."

Miss Gray's radiant face danced before his mind's eye, but she was meant for an honorable lord, not a vicar with dubious morals.

After procuring a wooden ladder, Will returned to the others.

Lord Bradbury placed greenery on a windowsill and glanced back at Miss Gray. "How is this?"

"A little to the left," Miss Gray said.

Her mother stood further back, watching the interchange with unconcealed glee.

"Bring the ladder here, if you would be so kind, Mr. Berry," the rector said.

Will set the requested item near one of the columns and eyed the metal supports bolted to the pillars on either side of the altar. Good. All was ready for the candles to be placed for the Christmas service. Miss Gray moved like a dancer amidst the pews, her slender, yet curvy form softly contrasting with the stone walls. She was such a spot of cheer.

Raised to marry a lord. Not a vicar.

That same kicked-in-the-gut sensation returned. Muttering under his breath, Will followed the rector into the vestry to collect the candles. He hurried back, almost starving for Miss Gray's presence. As they worked, Miss Gray hummed *The Holly and the Ivy*.

Will listened to her sweet voice for a moment and couldn't resist joining in. Bradbury also sang with a strong bass that harmonized with the melody. Was there anything he didn't do well? Will indulged in some very un-Christian thoughts about the oh-so-perfect lord.

Mrs. Gray also sang, with a voice as lovely as her daughter's. After a moment, the cheery tunes lifted Will's mood. Standing on the ladder, Will added the extra candles needed for the Christmas service, then assisted in wrapping the columns as Miss Gray had suggested.

In less than an hour, they transformed the humble parish church into a celebratory Christmas haven, almost fit for a drawing room.

"It's perfect," Miss Gray exclaimed. "A pity we cannot hang a kissing ball."

Will choked and laughed at the outrageous statement. Honestly, he agreed. Lord Bradbury's eyes widened. Mrs. Gray shot her daughter a withering look.

The poor girl flushed and bit her lip, looking down. "Erm, I mean..."

Mr. Appleby didn't see the humor, either. "Adding such a pagan symbol as mistletoe would no doubt create a public outcry and possibly have me removed from my position."

Of course, if Will could get Miss Holly Gray beneath a kissing ball....

Ahem.

For all intents and purposes, Will had given his word not to pursue her. He reviewed his newfound resolve to cling to duty, to turn over a new leaf in life, and to please his family by bringing honor rather than dishonor to the Berry name. Keeping his word, duly given to a lady, fell squarely into that resolve. No more romantic fantasies about Miss Gray.

To help ease her embarrassment, Will said, "We have mistletoe aplenty at the castle." Quickly, he changed the subject. "Does it meet with your approval, Mr. Appleby?" He opened his arms and made a sweeping gesture.

The rector nodded. "You all did a fine job, didn't you? Thank you."

"You're welcome, sir," Will said. "We look forward to your Christmas service tomorrow."

Bradbury inclined his head. "We were happy to be of assistance, my good man. It was a pleasant diversion."

As they rode home Mrs. Gray said, "That was indeed an enjoyable way to spend the afternoon. And I'm certain, Mr. Berry, it was pleasant to spend some time in a little church similar to yours, was it not?" She bestowed a benevolent smile on Will before turning her focus to Bradbury.

"Indeed," Will managed to say.

"It is a charming church," Miss Gray said. "And decorated as it is, it will be a fitting setting for a service celebrating the birth of the Savior."

"It certainly will," Mrs. Gray said. She addressed Lord Bradbury. "Does Parliament meet soon, my lord?"

"This year our first session began in November, but we have taken a recess for Christmas, and will resume shortly."

"Do you look forward to the Social Season?" Mrs. Gray continued.

"Not as much as I likely should." Bradbury paused. "Does your family plan to come to London this Season?"

"Yes, indeed. My dear Holly shall have her first Season this year after Easter, unless she receives a marriage offer first, of course." She glanced out the window as if enraptured by the scenery.

"Is one forthcoming, then?" Will couldn't help but ask.

She smiled at her daughter. "Well, one never knows for certain. Holly is so beautiful, as you can see, and so accomplished, that I expect her to be snatched up very soon. Do you know she plays both the harp and the pianoforte? And of course you've heard her lovely singing voice. Oh, and you should see her watercolors!"

This was the first tactical error Will had seen her mother make. Normally, she played the understatement rather than this overt pushing. Miss Gray flushed and cringed and generally looked miserable to be the object of such profuse flattery.

As if realizing she'd done it rather too brown, Mrs. Gray added, "Forgive a mother for being grateful to be blessed with such fine children."

"How very proud you must be," Bradbury said politely before turning to face Will. "It appears several of us are for ice skating this afternoon. Will you join us?"

"Yes, I will. Thank you."

Will gave up trying to find reasons to justify disliking Bradbury. If the lord wanted Holly Gray, Will should be a gentleman and wish them well. The thought rattled around in his head, but his heart refused to consider it.

After Will's mother had encouraged him to begin seeking a bride, Will had penned a list of all the qualities he wanted and needed in a wife. Miss Flitter had matched a surprising number of them, so he'd pursued a courtship despite his unenthusiastic feelings about her. Last night, he'd reviewed that list. Holly Gray had matched every single one as far as he could tell. And his feelings for her certainly were enthusiastic.

But he'd assured Mrs. Gray that he had no designs on her daughter. To pursue the young lady now would be to break his word, even if it had been implied rather than specific. Keeping his word mattered more than anything.

Very well, he'd avoid Holly Gray as much as possible without appearing to give her the cut. He must resist talking to her or even looking at her. He must.

Of course, that included ensuring that she never discover who had kissed her, which meant he must continue an ungentlemanly deception.

.

Chapter Seven

For the third time the past hour, Holly slowly turned so her mother could examine her appearance. Holly smoothed a hand over her ball gown, a silver sarcenet silk creation with a silver netted overskirt and seed pearl trim. Ribbons the color of holly berries matched the ribbon around her empire waist. She felt at once elegant and reflective of the Christmas season. However, after two changes to her hair and adding pearl earrings, she feared she may never look presentable enough to leave her bedchamber. She held her breath.

Mama finally nodded. "Yes, that will do."

Holly's breath came out in a whoosh. She offered a grateful smile at her lady's maid who possessed the patience of a saint. Without giving any clues as to her thoughts, the maid bobbed a curtsy and left the bedchamber.

Mama folded her hands as she always did when she delivered reminders on how to snare a husband. "Tonight will cement Lord Bradbury's interest in you for the remainder of the house party. Remember, a confident lady with the right balance of charm and wit, coupled with proper reticence, will always capture a gentleman's attention—certainly far better than those who are overly flirtatious or silly."

"Yes, Mama." The pressure to live up to her mother's expectations awoke a dozen butterflies in her midsection and sent them into to a frenzy. Of course, if Lord Bradbury had, indeed, kissed her, earning his good opinion could lead to more heart-stopping kisses, which increased Holly's motivation to make a match with him. But if not, and it turned out to be a ghost...

Her mother continued her pre-social event reminders. "Remember to wait for him to approach you. Do not even look at him until he does. A flower never chases the bee."

"Yes, Mama."

Her mother touched her arm. "And do not fret, my dear. You are a rare beauty—any man would be pleased to have you on his arm."

Holly tried to smile despite the winged insects cavorting in her stomach.

"After dinner, while we await the arrival of the guests coming for the ball, you should wander to the harp and play softly as if simply to amuse yourself. You might even do it before dinner. Later in the evening, when you have danced twice—not once only—with Lord Bradbury, offer to take a turn at the pianoforte so as to allow that person to have a turn dancing, even if she is only a simple village girl. It would be viewed as a thoughtful gesture on your part and a subtle way to reveal your skill."

Wryly, Holly said, "You seemed to have the evening well planned."

"Beauty and fortune aren't enough to snare a lord or a lord's daughter, you know—it takes cunning as well."

Cunning or conniving? But Holly held her tongue. Lord Bradbury seemed the perfect gentleman and Holly should be grateful for her mother's tutelage to attract his attention. But if Holly were honest, she far preferred the ease she felt when in the vicar's presence to the strain of trying to impress Lord Bradbury.

"Holly." Mama's voice took on a serious tone. "I have seen the way you look at the vicar. It's clear you are attracted to him."

Holly stilled. There were times when her mother seemed almost clairvoyant.

"But he is not for you," her mother continued. "His charm will wear off when you don't have money for candles or servants or pretty clothes, and when society's doors close to you. I do not wish that for you, and you cannot want that for yourself."

"In a country parish, society views won't matter

so much, will it?" Holly's voice sounded childlike and plaintive.

"Perhaps not as much as it does in a larger city where the *ton* gathers. However, I'm not convinced he is entirely circumspect—not as a vicar should be. He is a bit too cocksure, and, I suspect, a ladies' man—at least before he took up his profession. You want a true gentleman of honor like Lord Bradbury. You see that, don't you?"

Holly looked down and nodded. "Yes, Mama." Perhaps that aura of danger she'd sensed about Will Berry had been real. Mother's assessment of people often proved uncannily accurate. Despite rumor, rakes did not make good husbands.

Mama continued, "I am confident, if you will follow my instructions, that you will have engaged Lord Bradbury's affections enough that he will court you. Who knows? We may even garner a proposal before Twelfth Night."

"That soon?"

"I suppose if worse comes to worse, we could entrap him."

Alarm shot through Holly. "What?"

Mama peeped at her own reflection in the mirror and smoothed her hair. "You know, watch for a time when he goes off alone, and you can go in after him. Then I will arrive and be outraged that he was alone with you which would call into question your virtue. He would be honor bound to offer for you then."

Holly put a hand over her abdomen as sick dread turned her stomach. "We can't do that. It's wrong. And besides, such a tactic is beneath you."

Mama let out her breath. "Yes, I suppose you are right. I may be getting overzealous. Anyway, we needn't resort to such measures. Lord Bradbury is clearly interested in you. We have nearly a fortnight to secure a proposal from him, and you have clearly gained his notice. We will succeed."

Timidly, Holly said, "I'm not sure he's the one for me, Mama. I don't love him."

Her mother put an arm around her. "Love can come later, my dear, after you have made a careful choice. Never underestimate the power of respect and kindness. Lord Bradbury has all that and more. I am convinced, in time, you will see Lord Bradbury's fine qualities and fall in love with him as much as your young romantic heart desires."

Holly didn't just want to fall *in* love, she wanted to *be* loved, deeply, and for who she was, not for her ability to say and do everything exactly as she ought.

Still, perhaps Mama was right. Papa and Mama, who had a marriage of convenience, always acted lovingly toward one another, suggesting they must have fallen in love after marriage. Her brother Charles and her sister Ivy were clearly happy with their matches which Mama had managed. Holly ought to trust her mother more.

Holly said in a small voice. "Yes, Mama."

She trusted Mama. And if Lord Bradbury was her mystery kisser, she could fall in love with him after only a few more of those wonderful, romantic moments.

She was decided then. This evening she would search for a way to learn if, indeed, Lord Bradbury had kissed her. If so, she would turn all her energies to gaining his good opinion.

What if Mr. Berry were right about it being a ghost?

In the drawing room, Grandfather sat alone staring into the fire. He roused at their approach and his wizened face wrinkled into a smile. "Ah, Miss Holly. Do come sit by me, sweeting."

She obeyed him and perched on the footstool at his feet.

"Any more ghost sightings?" he teased.

Her cheeks heated but she kept her gaze as steady as possible. Did he see the truth in her eyes? "No, but then I have not repeated my visit to the conservatory."

"Ah. Wise, perhaps. You did seem a bit preoccupied after your encounter."

She twisted her fingers in her lap. "Yes, I suppose

I was." Now was her chance. She might ask him if he knew more. "Grandfather, what, exactly, happened when other people saw the ghost in the conservatory? Did they report anything, well, remarkable?"

"I only know of rumor. Some claim they saw a male figure walking among the plants. Others say a phantom stared out the windows. My brother claims a ghost tried to warn him away. My aunt said a transparent figure made romantic overtures."

She straightened. "In what way?"

"She never specified. But the spectre in the ballroom is much more interesting. She wails and moans and paces and even throws down her ghostly fan on occasion. Of course, the dungeon has the most ghosts, but according to family legend, they were rather of the violent sort. My grandfather had it sealed when a guest went ghost hunting and suffered such a terrible fright that his hair turned white!"

Holly gasped and put her hand over her mouth.

"He refused to speak of what happened."

Holly shivered. "Dreadful. But none of your other ghosts touched a living person?" Then, lest she be too obvious, added, "None of them are dangerous?"

"To my knowledge, none of our spirits have ever touched anyone." He patted her hand. "Not to fret, my dear. You are safe. And remember, many of our ghosts can only be seen by the light of a full moon on a winter's night. Most of the time, they're at rest."

A winter's night. By the light of a full moon. The moon would only appear full perhaps another night or two. Her family would leave long before the next full moon, and their departure would mark the end of her chance to learn the truth. She glanced outside, but clouds obliterated the moonlight. Would she ever have another moonlit night in this castle? She might never learn the truth.

"Holly, dear," her mother said. "Perhaps you ought to go play the harp. I'm sure Lord de Cadeau would rather have you play music than chatter at him."

Holly grimaced. She'd quite forgotten their plan to play the harp at strategic times. She peered up at the dear old man. "If it pleases you, Grandfather?"

"Indeed, play the harp for me, sweeting. Hearing you call me 'Grandfather' pleases me, as well."

Holly kissed one of his gnarled hands and strode directly to the harp. As she tuned the strings, she glanced at Lord de Cadeau. Had he viewed her action as cheeky? He sat with a serene smile curving his mouth, and stared into the fire. He certainly showed no signs of displeasure at her familiar gesture.

Beginning with her favorite harp pieces by Haydn, Holly played all the music she knew best. As other guests gathered, they spoke in hushed voices. Out of the corner of her eye, she spotted Lord Bradbury chatting with Joseph and Mr. Flitter. She focused on her music and played with accuracy. As she played, she lost herself in the music and let emotion guide her.

Mr. Berry entered. Odd how she felt him enter and not Lord Bradbury. Perhaps his footsteps were heavier to have alerted her to his presence. He greeted the others, his rich, musical voice carrying despite his soft tones. Oh dear. She was doing a poor job focusing her attention on Lord Bradbury rather than the vicar.

Lord Bradbury approached her. "Do you know any Christmas anthems, Miss Gray?"

She continued plucking her strings. "I do. Any requests?"

"Do you know *The Boar's Head Carol* perchance?"

"I know three arrangements of it." For some reason, her gaze strayed to Mr. Berry. Perhaps he had a beloved carol, too. She must ask him.

Lord Bradbury inclined his head. "I look forward to it."

She finished her current piece with a grand arpeggio. Miss Flitter scowled at her, probably irritated that Lord Bradbury had approached Holly instead. Lord Bradbury stood nearby, awaiting the requested song, so Holly launched into her favorite version of *The Boar's Head Carol.*

Once she completed the piece, she glanced at Lord Bradbury. With his hair styled to perfection, his snowy cravat tied with precision, and his fashionable superfine tailcoat, he created an image of lordly elegance. Tall and lean, with shoulders wide enough to suggest masculine strength, he should leave her pining for his attention.

He inclined his head again. "My thanks, Miss Gray. That was lovely. It is a particular favorite of my sister's."

"I hope I did it justice, then."

"Indeed you did. Thank you again." He bowed and returned to Joseph's side.

Wearing a triumphant smile, Mama made a gesture for her to continue playing. Holly played until they went into dinner. Seated between Lord Bradbury and her father, she removed her evening gloves and laid them over her lap. Mama glanced between Holly and Lord Bradbury, her expression serene, but she eyed the young lord like a hungry falcon tracking a sparrow.

Mr. Berry caught Holly's gaze. Her mother's admonition rang through her again. Besides, she must learn if Lord Bradbury had indeed kissed her. He might be secretly shy and now awaited signs of her interest before he told her he had kissed her. Surely, he would explain why he'd left her alone in the conservatory without revealing himself. It still seemed outside his character but more likely than a kissing ghost. Still, Grandfather had said the conservatory ghost had made romantic overtures to his aunt...

Giving Mr. Berry a polite nod, she turned all her focus on Lord Bradbury. As she sipped her wine, she tuned into the sound of his breathing, the rustle of his clothing. How odd that she could sit so near such a handsome and perfect gentleman—a lord with all the right connections—and feel little more than a passing desire to impress him for her mother's sake. Perhaps she needed only to get to know him better. Surely then she would fall in love with him.

She moistened her lips. "Did you enjoy ice skating this afternoon, my lord?"

Lord Bradbury glanced at her. "Yes, it was an invigorating and excessively diverting afternoon. The good vicar here put us all to shame, however."

She resisted the pull to look at Will Berry at the other end of the table.

Lord Bradbury added, "Pity you didn't join us."

"Oh, I haven't skated in years." She paused, leaping over happy memories of skating with her brother and sister, and children from their village. "What other pastimes do you enjoy?"

"Much of my time is consumed with matters of estate or Parliament, but I do enjoy the occasional game of chess or billiards, as well as fencing and riding." It all sounded rather ordinary, like the expected pastimes of every other gentleman.

How could she ask him if he had kissed her in the conservatory? There seemed no graceful way to go about it. It would make him uncomfortable if he were unwilling to reveal himself just yet. Would he ever tell her? And why the delay? If it had not been him, her question would only incriminate her, resulting in losing his good opinion.

"What do you enjoy, Miss Gray?"

She pushed at her curls tickling her cheek. "I love music, and despite my mother's statement, I am only passably skilled at water color."

"Your harp playing is very pretty, and you have a lovely singing voice."

"How kind of you to say. Music gives me a great deal of pleasure. Do you play an instrument?"

"I am skilled at pianoforte, but I have no true talent for it. My last teacher compared my playing to that of an automaton." A mildly self-deprecating smile twitched his mouth.

Holly gave a gracious laugh. At least he was humble, no small matter for someone otherwise so perfect. She could very well imagine Lord Bradbury playing with painful precision but no emotion.

After that, they spoke of inconsequential matters.

She occasionally made comments she intended to be amusing, but Lord Bradbury only offered polite smiles. Perhaps he was more stoic than she'd noticed previously. Or he found her boring. Neither boded well. He could not have been the one who'd kissed her, could he? Surely not.

Of course, if he had been the one in the conservatory, perhaps she had yet to break through his reserve to discover a man who kissed with such tenderness and passion. Many people had layers to their personalities; surely Lord Bradbury did as well. Her tension wound up like springs in a clock as she searched for appropriate and interesting topics to discuss with the lord.

From the other end of the table, Mr. Berry chuckled, the rich tones a soothing balm to her nervousness. "So he said, 'You should try life on a navy frigate—it's less hazardous than navigating the shark-infested waters of society.'" He laughed.

Everyone at that end of the table joined in his laughter—whether due to the cleverness of the way he'd delivered his story, or because they couldn't resist his infectious merriment, she could not say, but she smiled in response. Before she could stop herself, she glanced at Mr. Berry. His face and eyes alight in mirth, he was one of the most handsome men of her acquaintance. Candlelight shone on his warm brown

115

hair, contrasting with the creaminess of his cravat tied in a carelessly stylish knot. Everything about him seemed warm and relaxed.

Next to her, Lord Bradbury moved with precision as he ate, the knot of his cravat a study in refined and severe perfection, and every hair on his head in place as if not daring to defy the requirement of order. Everything about him was controlled—rigid even. But he enjoyed ice skating and he was kind. And he kissed as if...

What if he hadn't kissed her? Could it really have been someone else? A ghost? If she placed all her hopes on her mystery kisser being Lord Bradbury, only to discover he wasn't the one, then what? The vicar had seemed convinced Lord Bradbury had not kissed her. Perhaps he was right.

Mentally, she gave herself a shake. The identity of the man who'd touched her heart in the conservatory mattered little; her family depended on her making a match with Lord Bradbury or someone like him. She ought to set aside her personal quest and focus on the important goal of presenting herself as the perfect companion for a lord.

After all the courses had arrived and been consumed, Ivy stood and led the way out of the dining room. Most of the house party dispersed for their bedchambers to prepare for the ball before the guests arrived.

Christmas Secrets

As Holly ascended the stairs, Mama called to her. "Holly, dearest."

She waited for her mother, expecting delight that Holly and Lord Bradbury had conversed so much during dinner. Mama's mouth pulled into a tight line and her brows drew together. Holly checked her step.

Mama leaned into her ear. "You must stop looking at the vicar."

"But I—"

"Lord Bradbury is your target; he is perfect. I will have all my children married to titles and you are no exception. Now put your tongue back into your mouth, and keep your focus on your goal. If he sees you looking at another man, he may believe your heart is engaged elsewhere and be a gentleman by stepping back. Do not fail me."

"Yes, Mama," Holly managed.

She all but bolted for her bedchamber. Inside, Holly stood fighting tears. It seemed impossible to please her mother. Her love was conditional upon Holly obeying every edict. What would Mama do if she learned Holly had kissed a mystery man in a dark room?

A naughty imp inside her perversely tempted her to tell Mama and all the guests in the castle about the kiss to prove...what? What would it prove?

No. No good would come of her rebellion. She

would do all in her power to appear the perfect match for the stoic Lord Bradbury. If that meant she'd never learn the identity of the man who'd delivered the toe-curling kiss, so be it.

Chapter Eight

Leaning against a column in the ballroom, Will scanned the guests as they arrived for the Christmas Eve Ball. The usual types of ladies always attended, no matter the host or location. There was the older lady still desperately trying to hold onto her youth and former appeal, a young reigning town beauty who may or may not get a rude awakening when she had a Season in London, a poor relation whose status only allowed her on the periphery of polite society, a few wallflowers, a sweet young thing whose overzealous Mama kept pushing her on every eligible gentleman in attendance—much like Holly Gray, in fact. None of those types of young ladies now arriving at the ball used to pique his attention; he typically gravitated to girls who enjoyed a flirtation or perhaps even a kiss with no promise expected—much like Phoebe Flitter. However, Holly Gray occupied an unhealthy portion of his thoughts.

He found the object of his musing across the ballroom demurely looking down while one hand touched a curl next to her cheek in a purely feminine and alluring motion. Her beauty set her apart from

119

the others, but this ceased to be the sole reason he continued to obsess over her. Surely the accidental kiss had not knocked out all his senses. What else drew him to her? He discarded the mental image of his list and how well she'd matched it. Phoebe had seemed to match it as well.

The reason for his attraction to Miss Gray hardly mattered. She was not for him, according to her mother—and to his promise. He might as well do what he could to make the evening enjoyable for others. For all he knew, his future bride waited for him against a wall. Besides, he'd promised Joseph's wife that he'd dance every set with the predominantly female attendees, and when Joseph's wife was happy, Joseph was happy.

Will pushed off the wall and approached the hostess. "Would you please introduce me to the young ladies over there?"

Mrs. Chestnut lifted her brows. "The wallflowers?"

Next to his wife, Joseph barked a sharp chuckle of disbelief. "They aren't your usual prey, Will."

"No, but now I am a vicar seeking a wife." Will gave a rueful smile.

Though Joseph and his missus awaited an explanation, Will didn't elaborate. He looked back at Miss Gray just as she placed her hand into Lord Bradbury's. The sight made him grind his teeth.

"Very well," Mrs. Chestnut said. "But let's be quick; Joseph and I are to lead the first dance."

She took him to the wall and introduced him to three wallflowers who practically clung together, blushing and stammering. Joseph and Mrs. Chestnut hurried to lead the first dance.

Will bowed to the plainest of the wallflowers, whose name he'd already forgotten, and held out a hand. "May I have the pleasure of a dance?"

The girl paled and looked behind her before stammering, "M-me?"

"If you would be so kind," he said in his best debonair voice.

The poor girl nearly swooned right before his eyes. He waited patiently, his hand extended.

"Go." Her friend gave her a little shove.

The girl swallowed and gave him her hand. He led her to the end of the line as the musicians struck up a cotillion. The wallflower could barely manage a single word during the dance. Will finally gave up asking her questions. As they moved through the formation, she stumbled and kept turning to the wrong person. Will did what he could to subtly guide her, equal parts pitying her and worrying that she would hurt someone or herself. Then he found himself briefly partnered with Holly Gray.

She looked up at him with wide eyes. Quickly,

121

she looked away as if the sight of him burned her. His mouth dried. All his senses locked onto her. The lightness of her step, the feather touch of her gloved hand, the bounce of her curls framing her face, the rise and fall of her chest as she breathed, even the sound of her breath, all drilled into him until all other sensation faded into nothingness.

He wanted to compliment her on her beauty, her gown, her skill as a dancer, but that would not do. Instead, he asked, "Are you enjoying yourself, Miss Gray?"

"Oh, yes, very much. I adore the cotillion. You?"

"Indeed."

All too soon they parted, and he returned to his partner before moving on to the next young lady. He performed the steps automatically, keeping his gaze on his temporary partners, all while awareness of Miss Gray wrapped more and more tightly around him. Once he and his partner reached the end of the line and waited until the dance pattern brought them back in again, he closed his eyes and forced in a breath, seeking anything else upon which to fix his focus. His partner. He ought to focus on her. He opened his eyes.

She bit her lip, staring down at her fidgeting hands. Did tears shine in her eyes?

Gently, he asked, "Are you well?"

"I'm sorry." Her breath caught in a stifled sob.

He touched her elbow. "Sorry for what?"

"Making so many errors."

"Not to worry. The cotillion is a complex dance. I often get turned around myself." He smiled but she didn't look at him.

Still twisting her hands, she drew a tremulous breath and shook her head.

"Come, we are about to be drawn back into the fray." He held out a hand.

"I...." She bit her lip.

"You can do it. I'll help you all I can." Poor lamb.

She sighed, nodded, and put her hand in his. He gave her an encouraging squeeze. The dancers next to them drew them in and they circled as a group, then danced with the person across from them. And so the dance continued, Will and his erstwhile wallflower working their way back down the line toward their starting point.

Holly danced nearby. Will steeled himself for the inevitable assault on his senses. But it was too late. She laughed, and all his nerves shot into full alert. Once again, the rush of awareness of her, of her breathing, her fluid steps as she wove in and out amidst the dancers, overtook him. He refused to look at her, fixing his attention on each person with whom he happened to be dancing at the moment. On the rare occasion when his shy partner managed to look at him, he offered an encouraging smile. Her faltering steps became more sure and she moved more easily.

When the first dance in the set ended, they caught their breath. His partner snuck a glance at him.

He leaned in. "I knew you could do it."

A glimmer of relief shone through. The second dance in the set, a country dance, came more easily to her, but dancing through the line to Holly Gray hacked at his composure. She studiously avoided looking at him, probably because her mother had forbidden her to associate with him, as she'd forbidden Will to associate with her daughter.

By the end of the set, Will had never been so glad to end a dance. He escorted his partner to the wall where he'd found her, bowed, murmured something polite about how honored he was to have the pleasure of her company and fled the ballroom. Since being appointed to his position, he'd made a point of drinking very little, but tonight he sought a more fortifying beverage than the watered-down rum punch and wassail served to the guests.

He aimed for Joseph's library. Inside, he found a few other gentlemen who'd briefly escaped the hazards of the ballroom, some playing cards, others simply conversing over their drinks. Will found it within himself to scowl at them for Ivy Chestnut's sake as he found the port and splashed a little in a glass. The liquid burned as it went down. Closing his eyes, he sucked in several deep, calming breaths.

He'd been attracted to young ladies before and enjoyed their company in various forms, but he'd always managed to avoid getting overly attached—even to Phoebe. He ought to succeed in remaining unmoved by a girl he'd only known two days, and who was meant for another. Perhaps she was simply the lure of forbidden fruit. And a vicar, of all people, ought to be capable of avoiding forbidden fruit. He could. He would.

With another irritated glance at the gentlemen who clearly had no concern for the needs of ladies at the ball, nor for the hostess who had fretted over her guests' enjoyment, Will headed back toward the ballroom.

Young Rudolph Flitter came around the corner and entered a sitting room. In the doorway, he stopped up short, spun around, and stepped out, his mouth twisted as if he'd tasted something unpalatable.

He met Will's gaze and jerked his head at the room. "You don't want to go in that room. My sister is in there with the footman again. She sure likes to kiss a lot of boys. I don't get it." He made another expression of disgust, then trotted off.

Will halted. Phoebe was kissing a footman? Again? That must have been where she had gone when she was supposed to meet Will in the conservatory. Come to think of it, she did seem to vanish quite a bit, probably for the same purpose. She had admitted to Will she enjoyed kissing. She probably met up with her pet footman the night she was supposed to have met Will. He should have known.

He let out a snort. For someone who went about kissing a great deal, she should have been better at it.

As he passed by the partially-opened door, he cleared his throat. A male's voice, then Phoebe's giggle, came in response. Will backed up several steps, then walked toward the door as if he were just now passing by.

The red-headed footman who attended Lord de Cadeau most frequently came rushing out, his eyes merry. He picked up a tray and went into the ballroom.

Phoebe came out next, smoothing her hair, her face flushed. She'd probably been doing that all along, even while encouraging Will, and later throwing herself at Lord Bradbury. Will couldn't believe he'd considered her worthy of courting. He thought he'd left behind his preference for that kind of girl further back in his past. From now on, he would be more selective about ladies he chose to court.

126

After giving Miss Flitter a dismissive glance, Will returned to the ballroom and made a point of dancing every set with a wallflower. As his partners blushed and fumbled, and other ladies cast both come-hither and shy, admiring glances, his world righted itself. Ladies found him attractive. His vocation changed none of that. He had his pick.

Restored to his usual aplomb, he flirted and charmed his way through the entire wall of wallflowers—ensuring that he never led his partner to the same dance line as Holly Gray. He never looked at Miss Gray. Except to find out what line to avoid. Or when he couldn't resist. And once when he discovered her looking at him. Who could blame him for being smug about that?

He almost smacked his own forehead.

As he returned his latest partner to her position against the wall, he passed an older lady whose nose lifted in the air and who wore a pinched expression as if smelling some unpleasant odor.

"Humph. You're nothing but a social climber. Everyone knows your father made his fortune in trade."

Will craned his head to learn the identity of the speaker and her unfortunate victim. Facing the older lady, Mrs. Gray stood with her head high, but her face had paled. Her usual serene expression never shifted.

Though Will had no love for the woman who treated him as if he were beneath notice, he could not stand such blatant rudeness or snobbery such as she now faced. Perhaps this sort of treatment was the biggest motivator for her zeal to marry her children to the peerage.

He put on his most debonair smile. "Ah, Mrs. Gray, there you are. Lord Bradbury was asking about you. I believe he wishes to seek your permission to ask your charming daughter for a second dance." Ignoring the other woman, Will reached for Mrs. Gray's hand and wound it around his arm. "I shall escort you, if I may. The viscount also wishes to ask your advice on what wine to serve for tomorrow's Christmas Day dinner." He glanced dismissively at the snob. "Excuse us, please."

The other lady stared at him with her mouth hanging open. Mrs. Gray accompanied him silently with all the grace of a queen, though her mouth and jaw were tight, and her hold on his arm revealed her tension.

When they reached the far end of the room, he bowed. "I hope you don't mind my interference, but I cannot stand such vulgar incivility. And I am sure it would distress Joseph to see his mother-in-law treated so poorly."

Stiffly, she said, "My thanks. But I did not need to be rescued."

A defensive maneuver, surely. He bowed. "Forgive my impertinence."

Despite her appearance of ingratitude, he had done the right thing. It might spare Joseph or his bride embarrassment. If nothing else, he'd performed a service for Holly Gray. The lady of his thoughts stood fanning herself, her eyes bright and her smile lighting the ballroom better than the candelabra behind her. *Forbidden fruit.* Will sought out the most beautiful young lady in the room, requested an introduction, and bowed low before her as he invited her to dance with him.

Miss Gray's occasional glance bored into the side of his head, but he kept his gaze firmly on his new partner as he led her through the waltz, and then sat next to her at supper. Will barely tasted the food and instead flirted with his dinner companion so as to appear to be enjoying himself. In return, she flirted with enthusiasm. It was almost eerie how similar she was to every other flirtation he once enjoyed but now found empty.

"Listen," said one of the guests. "Do you hear it?"

Conversation died down. Soft as a whisper, church bells rang out.

"It's midnight," Lord de Cadeau said. "Today is Christmas Day." He raised his glass. "Happy Christmas to all of you."

Glasses raised and a chorus of *Happy Christmas* rippled through the room.

"Peace on earth, goodwill to men," Will said.

He glanced at Miss Gray, radiant and smiling...at Lord Bradbury, curse him. He probably had no idea what a treasure sat next to him, bathing him with those smiles. Will collected himself and addressed his beautiful dinner companion, whatever her name was.

"I wish you a Merry Christmas," he said in a husky voice.

"And to you," she replied in sultry tones. She sipped her wine and eyed him through lowered lashes. He threw his whole energy into dividing his time between her and the lady at his other side, completely ignoring Miss Gray's occasional glances burning his face.

After dessert had been consumed, they returned to the ballroom. As Will stood, he gripped the back of his chair and took a breath. He'd never found flirting so exhausting. Of course, the strain came from avoiding staring at Miss Gray. After escorting his companion to the ballroom, he sought Holly Gray's location. A quick glance about the room failed to reveal her. Where had she gone? Will sauntered out of the room into the great hall. At the far end, a slim figure in a silver ball gown trimmed in red disappeared into the...oh, heavens. She'd gone to the conservatory.

Probably alone. A quick check out the windows revealed bright moonlight. She'd probably gone to seek the "ghost" who had kissed her. What had he done?

He had to confess, and hang the consequences.

After a glance around to ensure no one observed him, Will strode after her. As he entered the conservatory, he paused on the threshold. A sense of *déjà vu* seized him. A virtual garden of plants in every size, flowers that normally bloomed only in summer, small trees including citrus, and clusters of chairs each with tables and lamps filled the room. Along the end, a wall of windows revealed a snowy, moonlit scene.

With all the grace of a swan, Miss Gray moved among the foliage and furniture to a lamp. She leaned over and blew it out.

Will called her. "Looking for your ghost?"

Miss Gray let out a surprised squeak as she whirled around. "Oh, Mr. Berry. Erm, yes." She huffed an abashed giggle. "I do wish to know if there really was a ghost here the other night. It would simplify everything."

"In what way?"

"Well, Lord Bradbury has not declared himself, and the more I get to know him, the more I agree with you that he would not do something like this—" she gestured to the very spot near the windows where Will

131

had kissed her "—without asking permission, or at the very least, without disclosing his identity. No true gentleman would do that."

Will winced.

She continued, "And Lord Bradbury has proven himself every inch a gentleman."

Will leaned against the door jamb, so as not to enter the room where they might be discovered alone together and call into question her purity. "And if your mystery kisser ended up being a ghost, then what?"

"Well, I...I suppose..." she toyed with her fingers.

"You could stop wondering?"

Bathed in the glow of the lamplight, her cheeks colored. A smile, part sheepish and part impish, touched her expression. "It would put my mind at ease to know one way or another."

Would she be disappointed to know it was Will? And most importantly, would it change her preference for Lord Bradbury if she learned he had not delivered her first kiss?

She sat on a nearby bench next to a topiary. "I suppose it sounds absurd to you, but I really must know. I do not think I could rest until I know."

Now was his chance. "What if it was someone else? Someone you least expected?" He uttered the words without thinking, curse him for a coward.

She spread her hands. "At this point, everyone would be the person I least expected."

Apparently, she did not consider Will as a contender. Though that had been his initial goal, now it gnawed at him. He had to tell her, regardless. Mustering his courage, he pushed off from the door frame and took one step closer. "Miss Gray, would you be disappointed to learn—"

"Holly Marie Gray!"

Will pivoted on his heel as Mrs. Gray bustled in. She shot him a dangerous glare as she passed him. Under her breath, she said, "I can see that you are not a man of your word, vicar."

Will held up his hands. "I assure you—"

She ignored him. "Holly, get back into the ballroom immediately. Lord Bradbury is looking for you. It's the last dance."

"Yes, Mama." A sigh weighted Miss Gray's words. The picture of contrition, she stood and headed for the door behind Will. "Thank you for your aid, Mr. Berry. It was kind of you to ensure I was safe."

Despite her obedient posture, a quick quirk of her lips and a mischievous gleam in her eye came his way.

Will stifled a grin at her subtle show of spirit. He bowed to her. "I am happy to be of service, Miss Gray."

As he lifted his eyes, he hoped she saw the gratitude in his expression that she'd attempted to exonerate him.

Miss Gray left with a swishing of her skirts. It was all Will could do not to follow her.

Her mother remained behind and stared him down. "I am disappointed in you, Mr. Berry. Did you not give me your word yesterday that you would not pursue my daughter?"

Will stiffened his spine and met her gaze. "You misunderstand my intentions. I saw your daughter enter this room, and I came to inquire as to whether she was well. I am not attempting to press my suit."

Mrs. Gray narrowed her eyes but after only a few seconds, donned a serene expression. "I see." She paused as if plotting her next move in a game of chess. "I hope you understand my maternal protectiveness. Think of your own mother; doesn't she want the best for her children? That's all I want for mine. My other children married well. They have no fear that they might do without the daily luxuries to which they are accustomed, and they are now ranked highly enough to be accepted into all the best social circles—not receive the kind of cuts that you now know I am subjected to on a regular basis. Holly has great potential. She does not deserve to be viewed only as the granddaughter of a tradesman or the wife of a vicar. I am sure you, as a gentleman of honor, understand and will not put yourself in my daughter's proximity as you promised earlier. Can I count on you?"

Hot anger poured into his stomach and a twitch started in his jaw. Mrs. Gray's smooth snobbery knew no bounds. He bit back his first several responses, first to point out what a hypocritical social climber she was, then defend his family lineage, and finally explain his ability to provide well for a family.

No, he couldn't lash out nor even defend himself. She was Joseph's mother-in-law and the mother of a girl who he greatly admired. He'd best not burn any bridges by losing his temper and lashing out at her. Besides, if he could spare Holly the same kind of scene he'd witnessed Mrs. Gray endure earlier this evening, he ought to do his part.

He ground out, "Yes, madam."

After delivering a brief, curt bow, he turned on his heel and left the room. Would he always fight an inner battle to behave in a manner appropriate for a vicar and a gentleman?

Chapter Nine

Flush-faced and breathless, Holly arrived at the ballroom. She'd taken a terrible risk going to the conservatory tonight. Waiting until after the ball surely would have been more prudent, but when the bright, still almost-full moon finally broke free of clouds and shone in through the dining room windows, she'd acted on impulse. That might have been her only moment to give her "ghost" another chance to reveal himself.

Now she may never know, moonlit winter nights being so scarce, and the moon already waning. Worse, the merry and dashing Mr. Berry now knew the full extent of her obsession with discovering the identity of her mystery kisser. He must think her silly. Or fast. He was too much a gentleman to reveal his opinion, but his unease in the conservatory had been painfully apparent.

Holly stood near enough the dance floor to be seen and available to any interested gentleman, but not so near that she appeared desperate. She put a hand on her hot face. A pity she'd left her fan on the far side of the room where her mother had been sitting. Nearby lay a fan on a sideboard table. She fanned herself with it, letting her gaze drift around the room as dancers paired up. As the musicians struck up the music, Lord Bradbury bowed before an older woman and led her to the line.

Oh dear. Mama would be disappointed. Or furious. No doubt she'd blame Holly's absence for Lord Bradbury's choice in a partner.

Mama appeared next to her. "Why aren't you...?" her attention moved out to the dance floor. "Why is he dancing with that lady?"

Holly continued fanning. "Perhaps he asked her for a dance hours ago."

Mama sighed. "I thought sure he'd ask you. He was searching for someone. But he was very careful about not dancing with anyone twice. I suppose he wishes not to make his preference for you known just yet—so as not to put what he believes might be undue pressure on you."

"Or he might not have a true preference for me." Holly shrugged. She clearly had not yet developed much preference for him, either, or she would be disappointed.

"Well, you simply cannot sit out the last dance." Mama looked toward the door. A calculatingly sweet expression appeared like a comfortable mask. "Oh, Mr. Berry, there you are."

Tingles sparked through Holly's chest at the mere mention of his name. With the unaccountable aura of mystery that sometimes overcame him, Mr. Berry checked his step before entering the ballroom. His gaze danced between Holly and her mother.

Mama beckoned to him. "Do come stand with us, won't you?"

Mr. Berry put a finger on his chest. "I beg your pardon, madam; are you addressing me?"

Mama's controlled laugh rang out. "Of course, of course. Always happy to converse with a *man of the cloth.*" Some hidden weight landed on her words.

He raised his brows. His mouth lifted in an amused quirk, but something intense, almost angry, glittered in his eyes. Was he angry with Holly for being so obsessed?

He fisted one hand and purposely opened it. "You want me to stand with you? To be in *proximity* with you and your daughter?"

Proximity? What was that all about?

Another controlled laugh came from Mama. "Of course, of course."

Holly tried to give him an innocent smile to prove she wasn't as fast as he might think after finding her alone in the conservatory hoping for another kiss from her "ghost."

Her mother gestured to Mr. Berry again. "I mean to speak with you, sir."

138

What in the world had gotten into Mama? A lady wasn't supposed to ask a gentleman to come to her. She was supposed to demurely await or, as a last resort, use the language of her fan to invite him to speak with her, a skill Mama had drilled into Holly.

She offered the fan to Mama and said saucily, "Here, try this."

Mama frowned at her impertinence but Holly only lifted her brows. For a moment, Mr. Berry seemed unwilling to honor Mama's request. Finally, he sauntered over with all the urbane elegance of a gentleman of leisure like those she'd met in the assembly rooms in Bath last summer. His formal bow almost smacked of mockery. Mockery?

"How may I be of service, madam?" He made a point of avoiding eye contact with Holly. A dangerous aura surrounded him, and she pictured him in pirate's garb, complete with an eye patch and a gold hoop in one ear.

Mama spoke in staccato. "It's the last dance."

His expression remained fixed, deadly, as if sharpening a weapon. "So it is."

In that same odd staccato, Mama said, "My daughter must not sit out the last dance."

Mr. Berry glanced about. "I do not see any prospective partners—every worthy gentleman in the room is already lined up."

Mama's smile hardened. "Except you."

That mockery in his demeanor thickened. "Oh, am I a worthy—?"

Mama cleared her throat loudly.

Holly glanced between them. Had they had an altercation? A knot twisted in the pit of her stomach. Had Mama warned off Mr. Berry the way she'd warned Holly to stop looking at him? That would be just like her. It explained his anger. Did this mean Mama believed he had true interest in her?

Was she right?

The knot evaporated into a hundred sparks as she admired the line of his jaw, the breadth of his shoulders, even the shape of his mouth. Would kissing Will Berry be as life-changing as kissing her mystery man—ghost?—in the conservatory? How odd that his nearness evoked all sorts of startling reactions in her that never occurred in Lord Bradbury's presence, even when the lord stood closer than Mr. Berry's present location. Her lips tingled. Her chest tingled. Her toes tingled.

Mr. Berry inclined his head in another bow. "Far be it from me to be derelict in my duties as a gentleman." He turned to Holly.

She swallowed through a dry mouth under the force of his gaze.

His expression softened into something she

hoped she might accurately identify as affection. Or, at the very least, kindness. His words, however, seemed forced and overly formal. "Miss Gray, would you do me the great honor of gracing me with your company for this, the last dance?"

Holly gave him her friendliest smile. "It would be my genuine pleasure, Mr. Berry. Thank you."

He held out a hand, his mouth fixed in a grim line. Holly glanced at Mama, caught her eye, and gave her a hard stare. Mama only lifted her chin and touched her hair as if ensuring it remained obedient to her wishes. Mama was always controlled. In many ways, she and Lord Bradbury had much in common.

Mr. Berry led her to the end of the line as the country dance began. Holly and the other ladies curtsied to their partners, who bowed. When they danced forward to their partners, she took his offered hand. A tickly sort of prickle raced outward from his touch, shot up her arm and landed in her chest where it burst into a thousand little lights. He fixed his attention on her, his eyes never wavering, that hard glint remaining.

As they circled, hands clasped, she said in a voice only he would hear, "Are you looking at me like that to spite my mother who seems to have issued some sort of warning, or are you trying to make up your mind about me?"

His brow lifted. She angled her head and gave him an impertinent smile. The hard edges of his mouth softened. Then he smiled. Finally, his eyes crinkled.

"*Touché*, Miss Gray. You seem to be remarkably good at reading me."

They danced back into their places before coming together again and circling the other direction.

"I apologize about my mother. She's very..." What word might not sound as if she were criticizing? "...protective. She has my best interests at heart, but I cannot always like her methods."

The humor left his eyes. "I'm sure she means well. It's only fitting that a mother wants what, or who, is best for her daughter."

"I respect her experience and wisdom. However, we do not always agree."

The hard line returned to his mouth. "Perhaps she thinks you are too young to know what is best."

"I do not claim to be worldly or exceedingly knowledgeable, but her priorities are different from mine."

They backed into their original position. Following the beat of the music, they marched forward to take each other by both hands. Her attention, nay her entire being, focused on his shapely mouth.

He parted those beautiful lips to speak. "Her priorities, I am sure, are based on her upbringing and experiences."

How noble of him to defend her mother who'd clearly insulted him. "She thinks a lady cannot be happy without a title and wealth and all of society inviting her into their drawing rooms. I think I cannot be happy without love based on mutual respect. And my definition of wealth is considerably different than hers."

"No vicar was ever accused of being wealthy, and more than thirty people would have to die before I'd inherit a title, nor do I wish for such a burden. Clearly, I do not match her definition of a fitting suitor." Resentment and another emotion she could not hope to name narrowed his eyes.

Had he been speaking of himself as a potential suitor, or making a general statement about how other mothers might view him? "That doesn't matter to everyone."

The dance sequence took them apart and they were obliged to dance briefly with other partners. She could hardly tear her gaze away from the graceful confidence of his every move.

When they came together again, she asked, "What, exactly, did she say to you?"

His postured stiffened. "I ought not speak of it."

"Let me guess; she wants what is best for her children, which includes wealth, titles, and invitations to every ballroom in the *beau monde*. Therefore, you are not on the menu?"

He let out a startled laugh as she'd hoped. "Menu?"

"The marriage café menu." Though she jested, it really wasn't funny. It was sad. Mercenary. And all too true.

He gave no reply—all the confirmation she needed. Holly had never guessed the full extent of how far her mother would go to manage Holly's life and her future until now.

Holly continued, "Then, after warning you to keep away, she had the audacity to bully you into dancing with me." She let out her breath. "I am sorry."

A kind, faintly pitying look came in response.

They separated again and she danced with her new partner, impatient to return to Will. When at last she could return to him, she asked quietly, "You didn't make any promises to her, did you?" Oh, dear. Was she being too obvious in her admiration of him and of her hope that he held her in high regard as well?

That intense look returned. "I did imply a promise of sorts." He glanced away. "As a gentleman, I should respect a mother's wishes." Following the

144

pattern of the dance, he promenaded with the lady next to Holly.

His words stung. He did not want her badly enough to risk her mother's displeasure. Perhaps he did not want her at all.

She huffed. Really, she was rushing things. They'd only known each other for a few days. Surely, an insufficient amount of time had passed for him to decide whether he wished to court her.

Of course, he had been put out by her mother's warning which implied he had formed an attachment for Holly. Didn't it? Perhaps he was such a gentleman that he honored a parent's wishes over his own. Or he had decided Holly wasn't worth the effort.

How very vexing that she could not divine his feelings for her! It was almost as vexing that she had yet to learn who had kissed her. Honestly, if she never found out, the experience would haunt her all her life.

As they circled, he asked so softly that his words almost failed to reach her, "You are displeased that I've decided to respect your mother's request?"

"You must do what is in your best interest."

"I am trying to do the right thing. For so much of my life, I've done the wrong thing, the selfish thing." A haunting sorrow entered his dark eyes.

Gently, she said, "I find that difficult to believe. You are a vicar."

"I wasn't always a vicar." A wry smile touched those beautiful lips and the sorrow in his eyes lifted but did not entirely leave.

They danced with other partners, leaving Holly hungry for his touch. When he came back to her, she said, "I used to do the right thing without question. Of late, I've been wanting more and more to do what is wrong. Sometimes I want to be bad, just a little." Like pin back the curls around her face and ice skate when the pond freezes and drink chocolate instead of tea.

He arched a brow. "Being bad is not all it's touted to be."

"Being good is not all it's touted to be."

They grinned at each other. His smile took in a secretive, dangerous edge. It transformed him into a rogue that made it all too easy to believe he might have been something of a rake in his school days before he matured into a kind and sensitive gentleman. He certainly had the Byronic good looks any female would be hard-pressed to resist. Her mother had sensed he had a checkered past. Still, everyone made mistakes; anyone could change if they truly desired, and he had surely turned into a fine gentleman, whatever else he might have been previously.

The first dance in the final set, ended. Holly and the other ladies dancing curtsied to their bowing partners. While the musicians paused to give the dancers a moment to catch their breath, Holly focused on Mr. Will Berry. Dancing put color in his cheeks and the sparkle back into his eyes. The dangerous rogue vanished and the charming gentleman returned. Such different facets to his personality gave him an intriguing depth.

She lowered her voice. "Thank you for dancing with me, despite the circumstances. It was extraordinarily kind of you."

If only he cared enough about her to find a way to court her, despite her mother's feelings, she might be tempted to give her heart to him, her mother's wishes notwithstanding.

A slow smile spread across his mouth and broadened to that roguish grin she was growing to adore. "Kindness wasn't my motivation."

His grin instilled a sense of daring—and hope. "Oh? What, pray tell, was?"

His eyes glittered. "A taste of forbidden fruit."

All the moisture in Holly's mouth abandoned her. If she were required to sing now, she'd never mange it. His lips drew her gaze and she superimposed her mystery man in the conservatory with him. If she never learned the truth, she would simply have to imagine William Berry as the man who'd kissed her and changed her forever. It would probably be a better solution to her mystery than the truth.

Chapter Ten

Will batted away the urge to lure Holly Gray into a dark room and confess he'd kissed her, preferably in the form of a demonstration. That would also spite her shrew of a mother.

But no, he'd vowed to act the gentleman. Following selfish instincts went opposite that vow. Besides, it wouldn't be fair to either Miss Gray or Lord Bradbury, who seemed to have formed an attachment.

Still, something had shifted in her expression. In someone less innocent than Miss Gray, that expression might have meant...well, hunger.

He cleared his throat and quieted his ridiculous imagination.

When the second dance in the set began, Will changed the subject to lighter matters. "Your harp playing was beautiful."

She smiled. "Did you enjoy it?"

"Very much. I seldom have the opportunity to hear harp music."

"You love music, don't you?"

"Yes, I truly do. I owe that to my mother, I suppose. She sings often and plays the violin."

148

"You have a fine singing voice."

"As do you."

They smiled at each other and spoke comfortably of light topics as the dance steps allowed. In her company, an unexplained wholeness overcame him. He had never felt such a sense of home before.

Near the end of the line, when they came together, holding right hands and dancing in a tight circle, she sobered.

Miss Gray looked him straight in the eye. "Do you really think there was a ghost in the conservatory? Truly?"

He broke out in a cold sweat. It was time for the truth—a portion of it anyway. The full truth must wait for a private moment so she could be appropriately angry without witnesses. She would probably deliver a well-deserved slap.

"I have never seen anything that would give me reason to believe ghosts are real, but there have been so many reports of such beings—even in this very place—that one would be arrogant to discount the possibility." He let out his breath. "However, in your case, I do not believe it actually was a supernatural being but rather one of flesh and blood."

She nodded. "I believe you are right. Still, I cannot completely discount the possibility." She turned to share dance steps with her new partner.

Will gritted his teeth. Somehow, he must find a moment to confess his transgression.

When she returned to him, they did one final set of steps and returned to their place in the dance line. He swallowed. "The truth may disappoint you."

"Perhaps, but at least I can stop wondering."

The dance ended as they bowed and curtsied to one another. He held out a hand. "Thank you for the dance, Miss Gray."

"Thank you for your gallantry, Mr. Berry."

Gallantry. So little about him qualified as gallant. As he escorted her toward her mother, he murmured. "May I—"

"Come, Holly." Her mother appeared. "Thank you, vicar. Your services are no longer required." She whisked away her daughter before Will uttered a word.

Will fisted his hands, then deliberately relaxed them. Impossible woman. There seemed no way to win her over. With a calm he did not feel, he sauntered to the far wall, trying not to look like a kicked dog. Somehow, he had to tell Holly. But how to get a moment alone with her—especially now that her mother had forbidden him to spend time with her?

Guests bade each other and their hosts goodbye. Giggles erupted as some passed beneath the mistletoe ball. A few ladies deliberately stood beneath it and received their kisses. The gentlemen who bestowed the kisses, plucked off white berries. Many berries vanished from the mistletoe.

If only Will could get Holly Gray beneath that kissing ball and enjoy one last kiss before he revealed his part in the conservatory and risked her cutting him for the remainder of the Christmas season.

He could, of course, tell her near the end of his visit so as not to face the loss of her good opinion of him. But there were too many reasons why he should not even consider such a course of action, or inaction, as the case may be.

As the last of the local guests left and all the members of the house party headed to their beds, Joseph summoned him. "Will. Do join me for a late drink."

Will ambled after his friend to his private study and plopped into an armchair next to a fireplace where little more than embers glowed. Joseph poured them both a drink and handed one to Will before taking a seat nearby.

"So, have you decided what you are going to do about my sister-in-law?"

Will snapped his head up. "I beg your pardon?"

Joseph grinned. "I'd bet my prize hunting hounds that you are smitten with her."

A choking half-laugh wrenched out of Will.

Joseph was not finished. "I've never seen anyone try so hard to ignore another person. And when you danced with her, I thought you were going to set the room on fire."

Will sipped his drink, rejecting every word that came to his mind.

"You, my friend, are very conflicted," Joseph said.

Will glared at the fire and changed the subject. "It seems your cousin has formed a preference for Lord Bradbury."

"I didn't know she was so fickle. Or shallow. At first, you two seemed so well suited that I thought you'd offer for her by the end of the visit. But now...." He shrugged. "I'd apologize for her behavior but it's clear to me you now prefer Holly, and she seems equally enamored with you. So, what is the trouble? Her mother?"

Will nodded and looked down at his clenched hands. "She warned me off. Apparently, I'm too low for consideration."

"My mother-in-law has very specific requirements for her children. In the end, however, it is Holly's good opinion you need—and her father's."

Will finished his drink and set it down. "Mr. Gray probably won't give permission if his wife is so set against me."

"My father-in-law is a good sort. He is fair-minded. Though he is quiet, when he takes a stand he is immovable. Not even his wife will sway him. I've seen it."

Will looked at him then. "Do you think he'd be willing to allow me to court Holly?"

Joseph shrugged. "I think he likes you."

Will huffed out another half-laugh. "What makes you say that? We've hardly exchanged two words."

"He sang with you when we were pulling the Yule log and walked next to you the whole way. He's also positioned himself near you often."

Will waved his hand. "That hardly signifies."

"All I can say is that it may not be hopeless. But, as the saying goes, '*faint heart never won fair lady*.' You must act. Do it quickly or someone else will beat you to the punch."

"I more or less gave Mrs. Gray my word—twice—that I wouldn't pursue her daughter."

Joseph studied him soberly. "Then you have a dilemma."

Will leaned over and hung his head. "I do."

He had heard of matters of the heart being at odds with matters of honor. He'd never suspected he himself would face that conflict.

Chapter Eleven

Following Christmas service at church, Holly walked behind the group. She inhaled the sweet, crisp air and watched the puffs as she exhaled. A heavy cloud cover, all the soft greys of river stones, dimmed the sun.

Young Rudolph Flitter led the way, surrounded by a herd of children, all excited for the Christmas feast and gifts awaiting them. Behind him walked Joseph's sister, who, along with her husband and four children, had finally arrived during the ball last night. Due to their fatigue and the lateness of their arrival, they had gone straight to their beds. Today, the little ones brought an element of delight to the special day as they had sung outside bedchamber doors to wake everyone, and giggled with the exuberance of their ages. Throughout breakfast and their walk to church, their merriment brought smiles to everyone's faces.

This morning, the little ones ran or skipped to keep up with Rudolph's long strides. Rudolph pretended to find them a nuisance but teased and encouraged them. Together they sang in a disharmonious chorus only youthful palates could make charming.

Would Holly have a family such as these little angels such as these someday? How she longed to tell stories to her own small ones, and teach them to read and make music, and sing with them indoors on winter's days.

Behind the children, their parents strode, occasionally calling out to them to stay in sight. Ivy held hands with Joseph. Lord Bradbury walked between Joseph and Miss Flitter who still blatantly tried to flirt with him, but he gave her little to no encouragement. Holly almost pitied him to be the object of such an obvious and annoying girl. Really, he deserved better. The lord was a fine gentleman. Distinguished, well spoken, handsome, and with a coveted pedigree. Lord Bradbury seemed to epitomize everything she should want in a suitor. Yet being in his presence gave her no special joy. He was too controlled. Too stoic. Too perfect.

Mama walked next to Ivy, often raising her voice enough for Lord Bradbury to hear her. Their exact words failed to reach Holly, but she hardly cared what they discussed.

Will Berry strode next to Papa. Somehow, he'd gotten Papa to talk, something few others managed to do beyond a word or two. Mr. Berry had kept his distance from her today, not even looking at her. A man of his word who honored a mother's wishes.

That should earn Holly's approval and respect. Instead, it left a hollowed out place inside.

Mr. and Mrs. Flitter dissected the Christmas service and criticized the rector. Then they complained about the cold and the unfairness of having to walk to church to satisfy some silly law. They paid no attention to their children nor made any attempt to stop their daughter from making a fool of herself. Holly should be happy her parents were always so pleasant in the presence of others, and had taught her how to comport herself.

Holly brought up the rear of the procession. Oddly melancholy and detached, she had stopped trying to put herself into the festivities. It all seemed to take place at a great distance. Going to church had brought her some comfort, and the service had been lovely. She'd admired the greenery she'd helped put up to decorate inside. But her awareness of Will Berry, and his obvious determination to keep his distance, had dimmed her usual enjoyment.

"Christmas is supposed to be a happy occasion." Ivy's voice snapped her out of her thoughts.

Holly lifted her head and blinked at her sister. "I didn't see you there."

"No one should walk alone on Christmas, so I waited until you caught up."

"Thank you," Holly murmured.

"What has you so glum today? Mama?"

Holly looked at her in surprise, both by Ivy's interest in her and the question itself.

Ivy continued. "It's clear to me that you and Will Berry have formed an attachment for one another. Joseph told me Mama warned him off, and being an honorable man, he's doing his best to comply."

Glaring down at her feet, Holly said softly, "I wish he wouldn't."

Ivy nodded. "It's a quandary. We want men to be honorable, but we want them to love us so much that they'll defy everything to be with us. When we are with them, we are happy and nervous and try to make sense of everything they do and say. When we are apart from them, we miss them so badly that we cannot seem to take joy in anything else. Does that about sum it up?"

Holly gazed out over the snowy landscape. Somehow, she'd grown comfortable with Will Berry— to the timbre of his voice, his animated expressions, the many facets of his personality, the warmth of his smile. If she must be honest, only he had brought to life so many strong and exciting sensations.

Finally, Holly admitted, "When I'm with him, I'm so happy. His absence leaves an emptiness inside that I can no longer discount. How is it possible that I could miss being with him so keenly? I haven't known him long."

Ivy smiled. "It happened that way with me when I first met Joseph."

Holly raised her brows. "I thought you said he was a pompous boor."

"I was trying to deny my feelings for him because Mama insisted on pushing us together the way she is trying to push you and Lord Bradbury together. But that's not what you are doing with Lord Bradbury, is it?"

"No. I looked forward to meeting him."

"You have always been better than I. I was so willful. I'm sorry for teasing you about always being so good."

"I do try, most of the time. And I do like Lord Bradbury. But there's something about Will—erm, Mr. Berry, I mean—that...that makes me so..." Her voice trailed off and she huffed. "It doesn't matter, I suppose. I am just going to have to stop caring for him somehow."

Ivy laughed. "I wish you luck, little sister."

They reached the castle and tromped inside. Ivy rejoined Joseph, leaving Holly once again to walk alone. Her maid waited inside her bedchamber to greet and help her out of her wet clothes and shoes. After changing into a gown appropriate for an early dinner, Holly paused next to the fire and cast a longing glance around her bedchamber. How much easier it would be to remain here alone where she didn't have to feel so keenly how much Will Berry avoided her, nor to worry whether anything she said and did would please her mother.

Pleasing her mother had become something of a chore.

"Shall I fix your hair now, miss?" the maid asked.

Holly glanced in the mirror. Her curls at the side of her face that Mama insisted she wear to please Lord Bradbury had turned frizzy.

"Just pin them back out of the way."

Her maid lifted a hand. "Beggin' your pardon miss, but the missus said I was to keep the curls."

"There isn't time. Christmas dinner will be served shortly."

Her maid lifted her brows in a knowing glance but did as Holly bade. Once that task had been completed, Holly donned a shawl and reached for the door knob. It opened so hard that Holly leaped back to avoid being hit.

Mama bustled in. "What is taking so long? Hurry along and stop dawdling. Lord Bradbury must be noticing your absence by now."

Holly stifled a groan. "Mama, I hardly think he will mind if I am but a few moments more. Besides, I thought you wanted me to make a grand entrance."

Mama gave Holly quick glance and grimaced. "Your curls!"

"They went all frizzy, Mama. There wasn't time to dampen and re-curl them."

Mama groaned. "Fine, have your little rebellion this once but I warn you, young lady, do not spoil this opportunity. How are we ever to get invited to the Countess of Tarrington's soirees or to the queen's drawing room if you won't heed my words so you can marry a lord?" She grabbed Holly's arm and hustled her along.

Holly clenched her teeth and tried to keep tears out of her eyes as she hurried to match Mama's pace. Holly had always known her mother's ambitions were high. Today the truth stared at her; in her mother's thirst to climb the social ladder, she viewed Holly as her pawn.

They reached the drawing room where Joseph and Ivy's guests had gathered. Holly shrugged out of her mother's grip. Head high, she glided into the room and moved to the pianoforte to provide background music and give the appearance of obeying her mother. It would also serve to help her find something to do until she could truly gather her emotions.

As she laid out the music sheets, she blinked back her tears. Control. Composure. She swallowed and breathed deeply. Calmer, she glanced about the room again. Her gaze landed on Will Berry. His

160

animated expression and tossed brown waves contrasted with Lord Bradbury's solemn face and painfully immaculate appearance. With his brows raised and an impish grin, Will delivered a statement out of Holly's hearing. Lord Bradbury's expression lightened, and he actually chuckled softly. Seated nearby, Papa also chuckled. How remarkable that Will Berry had the ability to coax smiles out of two of the most stoic men Holly had ever met.

Papa stood and went to stand next to the other men, and the three of them chatted. Papa seemed to like Will Berry, even though Mama viewed him as beneath her ambitions.

Holly played sonatas softly, letting the music guide her to a sense of serenity. Could it be possible that Will's presence added to that calm?

The children played a game of blind man's bluff, their happy voices filling the room with cheer. Holly focused on the children and their pure happiness, until she no longer had the urge to weep about her mother's high cost of approval, and how little Holly herself truly must mean to her.

Dinner was announced. As Holly stood, Will Berry bowed before her, handsome and intense. That sense of calm from moments ago rippled with a kind of energy.

He parted his beautiful lips. "Our hostess has

asked that I escort you into the dining room, Miss Gray, if I may?"

Her calm evaporated. Holly cast a panicked glance around. Mama already strode out of the room on Joseph's arm. Joseph's brother-in-law, who had arrived last evening with his family, bowed before Miss Flitter. Papa attended Joseph's sister, Mary. Lord Bradbury escorted Ivy. Over her shoulder, Ivy shot her a triumphant smile. It appeared Ivy had decided to mix up dinner companions. It might further fan Mama's ire, but Holly had the perfect reason to accept. Every corner of her heart urged her to do so. After all, who would go against a hostess's arrangements?

A vulnerability touched Will Berry's eyes and he lowered his hand an inch. "Unless you—"

She rushed to speak, "It would be my pleasure, Mr. Berry."

He glanced at the doorway through which Lord Bradbury escorted Ivy. "I apologize, but I have never been good at playing second fiddle."

"You misunderstood my hesitance. I assure you, despite my mother's wishes, my heart is not engaged elsewhere."

He said nothing in reply. Had she been too bold?

Silently, he escorted her to the dining room. As he seated her at their assigned places, with Lord

Bradbury on her left and Will Berry on her right, she admired the table. In the center of the table, two Yule candles cast off the gloom in the dining room, shining like twin Christmas stars against the angelic white tablecloth. Silver branches held other flickering candles.

"I like your hair like that," Will murmured, his voice low and husky.

Her insides fluttered about like snowflakes. She touched her hair. "It's much less fussy. Those curls my mother prefers always tickle me to distraction."

"Then you should wear it like this more often."

Holly smiled wryly. "Not if my mother has anything to do with it. I thought she would have fits of apoplexy when I came out of my room with it like this."

"Ah, you are quite the wicked girl, aren't you?" he teased.

Miss Flitter's giggle trilled from further down the table, but they both ignored it.

"I suppose I do have a *small* wicked streak," she admitted. Her gaze locked with his.

"I'd be curious to see how deep that runs." A sultry quality entered his voice and something forbidden and darkly exciting glittered in his eyes.

The image of Will Berry replaced her memory of her mystery kisser. She imagined his lips on hers.

163

Heat rushed to her neck. She made a point of removing her gloves. Her voice shook. "I thought you said being bad isn't all it's touted to be."

"I thought you said the same thing about being good." Amusement lifted the dark allure to his tones.

"Perhaps they both have their places," she suggested.

He quoted, "'*To every thing there is a season, and a time to every purpose under the heaven.*'"

"Well said." They shared a smile.

For this special occasion, the children joined them for dinner, trying hard to be on their best behavior for the grown-up table. Their excited voices rose and fell. Holly ran a trembling hand down her skirt. Remaining seated and still while filled with such a tingly sort of energy made her jumpy, and yet, all she wanted to do was remain at Will's side—preferably closer.

The butler entered, flanked by two other servants. All bore a massive silver platter with a boar's head decorated with spices and lemons. A collective sigh went up from the diners. Also on the table arrived pheasant pie amidst a myriad of other special dishes.

From the far end of the table, sitting at Joseph's right, Mother glared first at Holly, then Will. Holly's reckless courage of a moment ago fled. With a steadying breath, she turned to Lord Bradbury on her other side. He had engaged his dinner companion in conversation and hardly spoke to Holly. She waited. Perhaps he would address her. She refused to speak to him first. After all, her mother had counseled her to wait for Lord Bradbury to speak to her before engaging him in conversation. She was being perfectly obedient. She glanced at Will. Well, almost.

Topics at the table centered around everyone's most memorable Christmases, for good or ill, and family traditions. Twice, her gaze collided with Will's. Did she imagine the longing in his eyes?

Her heart swelled in response. She felt trapped between two worlds. Her mother and Lord Bradbury occupied one; Will Berry resided in another. Did she dare fully defy her mother and encourage Will? And more importantly, did she cast off her mother's restrictions and embrace her own likes and preferences, such as how to wear her hair, whether to drink tea or chocolate, and even if she might go ice skating?

Dessert arrived, including minced pie, frumenty, and Christmas pudding. Wassail and spiced wine also graced the table. Holly picked at her food, all her focus wound up in Will's scent, of the quality of his breathing, the warmth of his body so near. His left hand brushed against hers beneath the table. His glance slid her way. She tried to disentangle herself

165

from his gaze for propriety's sake, but finally gave up and just looked at him.

His mouth turned up on one side and he finally looked away to where he toyed with the stem of his glass with a long, elegant finger on his right hand. His left hand, still touching hers, moved closer, and he wound his pinkie around hers. Her breathing stuttered. The strength and warmth of his bare hand on hers, such an intimate contact, battered her resistance. If he had asked her to meet him alone in a dark room, she would have been hard pressed to remember why she ought to refuse him.

After enjoying the repast, Ivy, as the hostess, stood. "Shall we, ladies?"

Holly barely managed not to blurt out, 'Is it that time already?' Instead, she gave Will a helpless smile and removed her hand from his.

"Don't be long, my dear," Ivy called impishly to Joseph on her way out.

Joseph grinned as if they shared a secret joke and watched Ivy walk out. The affection in his expression tugged at Holly's emotions. How she longed to have someone look at her with such love.

Holly almost asked if she could remain next to Will. But that, of course, was unheard of. Yet the mere thought of leaving his company created a hole of loneliness, and her hand was suddenly cold without his touch.

Christmas Secrets

In the drawing room, Holly moved to the harp. Playing the harp required more concentration than the pianoforte, and again, it would appear that she obediently anticipated her Mama's wishes. However, the temptation to pick up a book instead—or better yet, find a way to have more moments alone with Will—beckoned to her.

Mama took a turn about the room with Ivy, her face serene but with that focused look Holly recognized as a covert scolding. Ivy shook her head, replied something Holly could not hear, and smiled as she patted her hand. Ivy stepped away from Mama and joined a circle of ladies sitting by the fire. Getting married had secured Ivy's independence from her mother's control. How Holly envied that.

Joseph's sister, Mary, and the Flitter ladies now sat together with Ivy, talking and laughing. Holly tuned them all out and focused on her music.

The gentlemen eventually joined them. The air changed with Will's arrival. Holly kept her gaze on her music lest she give into temptation to look at him. It also provided a good excuse to not be available to speak with Lord Bradbury. Conversations rose and fell around her. Miss Flitter's trilling laugh rang out. With a nursemaid keeping them organized, children played a game of snapdragon.

"I think I saw a book on that very subject in

Joseph's library," Lord Bradbury said to Papa. "I'll fetch it for you." He strode for the door.

Holly made the mistake of glancing at Will Berry. At that same moment, he looked at her. His mouth pulled up on the corners in a gentle smile. Did she imagine longing in his gaze or was that her own feeling? Her heart flittered about, both weighted and light. How she longed to stand at his side and bask in the warmth of his presence, to hear whatever amusing story had brought a laugh to both her father and Lord Bradbury. What would it be to feel his arms around her, to share a moment with him like the one she'd shared in the conservatory with her mystery man?

Was it possible, he was the one who—?

Mama appeared next to Holly and said in a voice loud enough for the room to hear, "Holly, darling, your playing is lovely as always, but do take a turn about the room with me." She placed an overly firm grip on her arm.

Mostly to keep the pressure off her arm, Holly stood. "Mama—"

"Walk with me," Mama whispered urgently. An expression closer to panic than Holly had ever seen on Mama's face brought her to her feet.

She would never understand the way her mother's mind worked. Still, she did not wish to cause a scene. She walked with her mother around the room.

As they approached the door, her mother tugged her out of the drawing room. "We must go to the library. Now."

"But—"

Mama took on an urgency Holly couldn't begin to fathom. "Quickly now. I believe Miss Flitter means to entrap Lord Bradbury. We must not let that happen."

Phoebe Flitter did indeed stride to the far end of the great hall toward the library.

Mama called, "Oh, Miss Flitter!"

The girl frowned over her shoulder, then charged through the library entrance. Holly and her mother dashed after her. They rushed in just as Miss Flitter launched herself at Lord Bradbury. He staggered back, dropped a book, and managed to catch the girl as she landed against him. Miss Flitter pressed a kiss to his lips.

Lord Bradbury grabbed her shoulders and shoved her away. "What the devil—?"

"Oh, Blake, you are so romantic!" she said in an overly high, breathy voice. "I love when you play these games with me!"

He took another step back. "How dare you throw yourself at me like a trollop. And I have not given you leave to address me so informally."

"Miss Flitter!" Mama scolded.

Miss Flitter tossed a coquettish smile over her shoulder at Holly and Mama, and smoothed her hair. "Oh my, I suppose we've been caught." She smiled up at Lord Bradbury. "Now you are honor-bound to offer for me, aren't you, darling? But you don't mind, do you?"

He paled.

As he opened his mouth to retort, Mama said sternly, "That is quite enough of this nonsense. We saw you throw yourself at him. Now leave before we reveal to the entire group what a conniving little hussy you are."

Miss Flitter shrank away from Mama, and tried to snuggle into Lord Bradbury. In an overly pleading voice, she said, "You aren't going to let her talk to me like that, are you, Blake?"

Pouting, she batted eyes at him that might have been beguiling if she hadn't been so obvious and vulgar. What had Will ever seen in her? He must have been taken by her pretty face and not seen her for what she was. He could not have known her well.

Lord Bradbury recoiled. "Leave off at once. And never address me by my Christian name. In fact, never speak to me again or I vow I will cut you, despite my friendship with your cousin."

Like an actress donning a role, Miss Flitter changed expression to one of hurt. "My darling!"

Holly folded her arms and glared at the little tart. "Your cheap plan to entrap Lord Bradbury has failed, Miss Flitter. I cannot believe you tried such an underhanded tactic."

With a cold stare fixed on Miss Flitter, Lord Bradbury commanded, "Leave at once."

Miss Flitter let out a huff and marched toward the door. As she passed Holly and Mama, she muttered, "You have ruined everything!"

They ignored her.

With deliberate calm, Lord Bradbury retrieved his book and stood gripping it with white fingers. "I am grateful to you both."

Smoothly, Mama said, "When we saw her follow you out, we suspected her goal. Of course, we could not let such an underhanded tactic occur."

Lord Bradbury shook his head. "Intolerable."

Holly shrugged off the memory of her mother even toying with the idea of trying the exact tactic which they condemned in Miss Flitter. It had, after all, only been an idle thought, surely.

"I hope this doesn't ruin your enjoyment of the season," Mama said to him. "I'm sure Joseph would be grieved were you to leave prematurely."

He let out a long exhale. "No doubt. My thanks, again."

Mama sank into a curtsy. "Shall we?" She gestured to the door.

Grimly, he nodded. Mama was all sympathy as he passed them and exited the room. Holly squared her shoulders, prouder of her mother than she had ever been. Her observation had saved a fine man from a decidedly awkward situation. She was a hero.

Mama gave Holly a triumphant smile. "Now he has an even better opinion of us. That works very nicely to our advantage."

Holly slumped. She should have known Mama's quick thinking had a different motive. "Mama, what you did was noble, and Lord Bradbury is most grateful. But please stop your machinations for once and let us simply enjoy Christmas Day."

Mama's startled hurt caught Holly by surprise. She regretted her sharp words, but her disappointment in her mother had destroyed all her earlier admiration. Holly returned to the drawing room to try to find a way to regain the mirth that should accompany Christmas Day.

Chapter Twelve

Will watched snowflakes fall outside the drawing room window. The children's delight at the Christmas candy and the gifts their parents gave them brought smiles to the faces of all the adults. The scent of the Yule log mingled with the greenery scattered around the room, creating a warm, festive feel that should have brought him more joy than it did.

He must somehow find a way to break down the barrier between himself and Holly Gray. If only he knew how to go about it. And when.

Next to Will sat Holly's father. Though normally quiet, he'd proven a surprisingly witty and thoughtful man. Will could plead his case to Mr. Gray. Perhaps he would be willing to at least consider allowing Will to court his daughter.

Mrs. Gray had practically dragged Holly out of the room not long after Lord Bradbury went to the library. Judging from their absence, Mrs. Gray had cornered the lord and was trying some new ploy to get him to notice her daughter. If only she'd stop trying so hard, she might attain her goal.

Not if Will had anything to do with it.

"Speak your mind," Mr. Gray said in his usual soft-spoken manner.

Will started. "Sir?"

"Something is on your mind. Out with it." For a man of few words, and staccato-style sentences, he managed to make his point.

Will glanced at the others. Lord de Cadeau launched into another story, this one about the time he'd fallen through the ice and his sister had saved him. Mary's children and the other adults in the room sat engrossed, occasionally interjecting exclamations or questions.

Now might be his best opportunity. Will picked up his courage like a sword and charged. In a low voice, he addressed Mr. Gray. "Sir, I admire your daughter. A great deal. But your wife has asked me to keep my distance due to my lowly status as a vicar. She desires a gentleman of rank."

Mr. Gray nodded. "Titles matter to my wife. Show up those who snub her. Make her father proud." He paused. "She wishes for more open doors for our children."

"I gave her my word I would step back, and I will keep it if I must. But I am reluctant to give up on your daughter."

The older man watched him without blinking.

"I think she returns my regard," Will added in case that mattered.

"I see you two." Nodding, Mr. Gray stared thoughtfully out the same window that had captured Will's focus a moment ago.

"Do I have any hope of changing your wife's mind?" Will asked softly.

"Not likely."

Will's heart withered. This was it then. If neither parent would give permission, what hope did he have?

Assuming Holly wanted him—a big assumption—they could elope, but that would terminate his position as vicar, disappoint his family, shame hers, and probably humiliate Holly. Besides, did he really want to marry her? Or merely court her to determine if he wanted to marry her, his list of wifely qualities notwithstanding? He'd been hasty with Phoebe; he would be wise not to rush this time.

He pictured introducing Holly to his congregation, working at her side with the parish children and the poor, creating memories together, spending his life with her, teasing her across the breakfast table, finding new ways to coax a smile or laugh from her, taking her ice skating, blending his voice with hers in song, creating Christmas traditions together, kissing her any time he wanted, waking up with her in his arms. His parents would adore her, as would his parishioners.

Sweet contentment crept over him, along with

longing. Yes, he wanted that. Very much. Was this love?

With a desperate energy, Will tried again, "Sir, I vow my feelings for her are both tender and genuine. I will do all in my power to bring her happiness. Isn't there any way I might be allowed to at least court her, to learn whether we suit?"

"My wife will not change her mind."

Will slumped.

"I have final say." A rare gleam of humor entered Mr. Gray's eyes. "A benefit of being head of the household."

"Sir?" Will hardly dared hope.

"I take it you are not entirely an impecunious gentleman?" The corners of Mr. Gray's mouth turned up into a semblance of a wry smile. It was, perhaps, the longest sentence the man had uttered since Will had met him.

Though hope was probably foolish, Will took courage from the question as well as the friendliness of the older man's expression. Earnestly, Will said, "No, sir, I am far from destitute. I received a small settlement when I reached my majority, and my uncle gifted me more when I received my degree at Oxford. Also, the living I receive as a vicar is not excessively humble and the vicarage is very modern and comfortable."

"I looked up the Berry family. Respectable. Noble. Well connected."

Will held his breath, afraid to hope.

Holly's father considered another moment. "An agreement between you and me would trump my wife's objections."

Will's pulse pounded in his temples.

Mr. Gray studied Will thoughtfully. The clock on the mantle chimed. The viscount's voice rose. The children gasped at the old man's story.

What else might Will say? Touting his many fine qualities seemed pompous, not to mention it would be a short list. "Sir, I beg you to give me a chance. Let me prove myself to you, to your wife. To your daughter."

Lord de Cadeau's voice fell, the listeners gasped, and the viscount delivered his ending. His audience laughed. Some applauded. Even the youngest child laughed and clapped, probably in imitation of the adults. Will eyed Mr. Gray but still the older man said nothing. Perspiration trickled down Will's back.

Lord Bradbury slipped in and handed Mr. Gray a book on a topic they'd discussed previously. "You may find this interesting." He paused. "Forgive me, but I believe I shall retire now."

They bade him good night. Thoughtfully, Mr. Gray fingered the book. Will held his breath. Had the

177

interruption destroyed any chance of Mr. Gray considering Will's request? How might he broach the subject again?

After an agonizingly long wait, Mr. Gray finally nodded. "You may court my daughter."

A weight lifted off Will's chest. He did not yet have permission to marry her. He still had to fully win them over. But at least now he had a chance. Will probably grinned too broadly but he couldn't help it. "Yes, sir, I understand. Thank you, sir."

Holly entered, beautiful, warm, enchanting. Catching his gaze, she smiled at Will from across the room. It was all he could do not to leap to his feet and rush to her side.

Under his breath, Mr. Gray said, "You love her?"

"I think I do." Will looked at Holly. Once again came that longing to be in her presence, to tease a smile from her, to immerse himself in that wholeness he only experienced in her presence. "Yes. Yes, I do."

Her magnetic pull tugged at him.

"Excuse me, sir." He arose and approached her. After a brief bow, he gestured to the pianoforte in the corner of the room. "Miss Gray, I believe a Christmas tune is in order. Would you be so inclined?"

Sun shining through an open window could not have warmed his heart as much as the light radiating from her face. "I'd be happy to, Mr. Berry. Would you be so kind as to turn the pages for me?"

He nodded and offered his arm. After moving out of Mr. Gray's earshot, Will said under his breath, "Is there room on the bench for us both?"

She pretended to consider. "Mmm, I suppose, but only if we sat very close."

That playful glance had an almost sultry quality to it. He sat on her left, so near that their thighs touched. Progressively hotter eddies swirled through him. Her scent of vanilla, cinnamon, and orange welcomed him like a friend. After removing her gloves, Holly opened her book of Christmas carols with trembling fingers. Did she shake from fear or excitement? As she set her fingers on the keys, he reached out and enfolded one of her hands in his. She went still.

Under his breath, he whispered, "Do you want me to move away?"

"No." She looked down. Color bloomed in her cheeks.

The sensation of touching her bare hand with his heated the eddies to a roaring fire. Still, he must take this slowly. He released her hand. "What are you going to play first?"

She turned her head and looked him in the eye, bringing her mouth within mere inches from his.

Instinct and need roared through him. But he couldn't kiss her. Not now. Certainly not here. He froze lest his baser urges get the better of him.

She blinked. How had he never noticed that rare blend of blue and green and grey in her eyes? Perhaps at dinner, the only other time he had been as close— aside from a dark conservatory—he'd been too focused on her mouth, and how badly he wanted a repeat of their first encounter, to notice her eyes.

She moistened her lips, re-capturing his attention. "Do you play at all?"

Hoarsely, he managed, "I do."

"Do you have a favorite carol?"

"I enjoy all of them."

She gave him a sideways glance as if she did not believe him, and thumbed through her music. "I have a duet for a German carol. Do you wish to play it with me?"

"I have a duet for a German carol. Do you wish to play it with me?"

"I can try but I do not sight-read well."

She smiled as if she did not believe him and thumbed through her music. "Here it is." She laid it out on the music stand.

Will turned his focus on the music. "It doesn't look terribly difficult. Should I play the lower part since I'm already sitting here?" He was less likely to butcher the easier line as he sight-read.

180

"Lovely."

Yes. Yes, she was.

"Are you ready?" She waited for him to answer.

He nodded and they placed their fingers on the keyboard in the same moment. Holly counted out the tempo for a full measure, and they began. Will stumbled through the first few lines. Finally, he shut out all other distractions to concentrate on the music. At least, he tried. Holly's spring-Christmas fragrance touched him on an elemental level. The warmth of her body so near heated him more than the Yule log in the hearth.

Shifting his focus to making music, he fell into a rhythm. He found a pattern in the broken chords, slowing to match Holly's more intricate part. They played as a team, unified. He could have this with her, this unison, this sensation of belonging to a greater whole—and not only while they played a duet on the pianoforte.

The last notes rang out and faded. Smiling, she turned her head and met his gaze. The middle of his chest turned to plum pudding.

Barely above a whisper, and with a strangely vulnerable expression, she asked, "Are you no longer under obligation to honor my mother's request?"

"Your father released me from that promise."

"Did he?" Her brows lifted and her lips curved upward.

He nodded. "Only moments ago. Something about his decision overruling hers."

Her lips twitched deliciously. "He seldom puts his foot down, but when he does, no one raises a question."

"I'll have to keep that in mind." He took her hand. "Holly, I—"

"Delightful!" Lord de Cadeau clapped his gnarled hands. "Now, come enjoy a warm drink. Sit beside me, sweeting, and you too, young Will."

The moment passed and Will let out a helpless laugh. Perhaps it was just as well he hadn't finished his statement. He needed to confess his actions in the conservatory before he declared his feelings for her.

He and Holly moved to the seats the viscount had indicated. Servants brought trays of bread, meat, and cheese as a sort of late supper, since Christmas dinner had been served in the middle of the day. Tea, chocolate, coffee, and wassail arrived as well.

Sipping his wassail in favor of his usual coffee, Will sat next to Holly, hardly able to swallow through his desire-charged energy. He might never eat or sleep again. Holly enjoyed two cups of chocolate, smiling as if she enjoyed a private joke. Dare he flatter himself that she was happy to be sitting so close to him?

After they'd eaten, Grandfather gestured to Will and Holly. "Won't you play some more? And sing, too?"

A smile crinkled the corners of Holly's eyes. She touched the back of Will's hand with her pinkie finger. "I will, if you will."

He wanted to kiss that playful smile. And all the rest of her.

As Will and Holly returned to their position at the pianoforte, someone let out a huff. Miss Flitter hovered nearby, shooting a glare at Holly and Will.

"I can play, too, you know." She pointedly sent Will the same flirtatious smile she'd given him at their first meeting that had piqued his interest, fool that he was.

He inclined his head. "Of course, Miss Flitter. I'm sure you'll have plenty of opportunity to regale us with your talent later this evening or at other times during the house party."

"I could play with *you*," she persisted. "Now."

Apparently robbed of Lord Bradbury's presence, she'd reverted to wanting Will's attention again. The fickle flirt.

"Perhaps another time," he said as graciously as he could manage.

"Play *I Saw Three Ships*," the viscount called.

"Yes, Grandfather," Holly said. A delightfully rueful smile accompanied her nod. She turned the pages until she found the requested song.

"You're humoring him," Will said.

"How can I not? He's such a dear old man."

"He is."

They played the carol, written as a solo, as a duet. Holly played the melody on the upper octaves and expanded it to sound fuller, while Will played the bass notes, adding to it when he could. They both sang, and their voices blended sweetly. Will could do this for the rest of his life. He intended to...if Holly would have him once she learned of his deception.

Chapter Thirteen

After she and Will completed their duet, Holly smiled at the children gathered around the pianoforte and gestured to the room at large. "Let's all sing the next one. Any requests?"

"*Hark, the Herald Angels Sing*," one of the children called out.

"As you wish, my dear," Holly said.

Miss Flitter let out a huff and flounced to the far corner where her parents sat reading and ignoring the rest of the party. Holly played the introduction to the carol. Children's voices, sweet and slightly off-key, blended with adults, some with better ears for pitches, and some even less in tune than the children. It created a happy chorus of holiday cheer.

Mama hovered nearby, unsmiling, her brow wrinkled. She was probably furious that Will had broken his vow to stay away from Holly. Normally, such a show of displeasure would have unnerved Holly and sent her begging for forgiveness. This time, Holly pretended not to notice. She had a mind of her own and would choose her associates and her suitor. If all went well, she might even choose her husband.

She allowed herself one more glance at Will. His gentle, secretive smile encouraged her that they were of like minds.

The guests sang carol after carol until their voices grew tired from singing. The little ones got fidgety, then fussy, and the nursemaid put them to bed. Adults gathered near the fire, talking in small groups. Rudolph amused himself with a kaleidoscope.

Holly sat next to Will on a settee, her fingers itching to touch his again. She was beginning to think she could she spend the rest of her life with him. Sitting so close to him created a sensation of familiar belonging, mingled with a nervous kind of energy. What would it be like to kiss him? Would it be anything like her experience in the conservatory?

She drew in a long breath. If only she could solve the riddle of who had kissed her that night, she might allow herself to give her heart away. It would be so ironic if her mystery man turned out to be Lord Bradbury.

Of course, there was still that mad notion that her kisser had been a ghost.

The only other possibility that she wanted to consider was that it had been Will. But surely he would have told her, if not at once, then by now. He was too honorable to facilitate such a deception, especially for so long.

She glanced outside. Great snowflakes drifted by, lazy and magical against a dark night. The moon was nowhere to be seen. A visit to the conservatory would be fruitless; there would be no likelihood of finding answers tonight.

As the fire burned low, Grandfather dozed in his chair. Ivy rested her head on Joseph's shoulder in marital comfort. How Holly longed to share such moments with someone. She glanced at Will. Beyond handsome, beyond that enticing pull she'd felt toward him the last few days, something else about him drew her. Each smile he turned to her, each song he sang, each conversation they had, all created a sense of belonging. She had no need to censor her words or her actions, she could be her genuine self with him, having no fear of rejection or the pressure to always do and say exactly as she ought.

The other guests stood or sat in small circles. Miss Flitter paced the room, occasionally casting surly glances in Holly and Will's direction. She finally plopped down on the window seat.

A footman served another round of wassail but Holly declined. Miss Flitter also declined, her mouth turned down. Holly felt little pity for the girl's sour mood. Miss Flitter had cast off a good man to throw herself at a lord, but seemed to want the attentions of both. Of course, after her shameful scene in the library, even she should know she had no chance with Lord Bradbury. Such reasoning probably drove her to make another try for Will.

Still, no one ought to feel low on Christmas. Perhaps Holly would be the last person with whom Miss Flitter wished to have a conversation, but Holly meant to try.

She excused herself from Will, arose, and joined Miss Flitter at the window seat. The younger girl eyed her with a mixture of curiosity and dislike.

Holly greeted her with a kind smile. "Miss Flitter, if I may, I hope you do not view me as your enemy. I assure you I did not act out of a desire to hurt you, only to protect an innocent man."

Miss Flitter let out a huff. "You did that so you could have him for yourself. But you want Will Berry, too. You always have to be the center of attention." She folded her arms.

Holly could say the same about Miss Flitter, but speaking her mind would not further her goal. "My mother hoped for a match between Lord Bradbury and me, but my preference is not for him." Holly reached out to her but didn't dare touch the girl who might not welcome the contact. "I hope you are not overset by my attachment with Mr. Berry. It rather caught me off guard, and you seemed to have no particular affection for him beyond an innocent flirtation." Perhaps *innocent* gave Miss Flitter too much credit.

Miss Flitter sniffed. "I thought he was in love with me. But he certainly seemed to get over me in a hurry."

"Much the way you got over him, I expect."

Miss Flitter waved her hand. "Oh, I was never in love with him. He was merely a diversion. He is very handsome, but I could never marry a vicar."

Holly ground her teeth. Miss Flitter was making it difficult to have any sympathy for her at all. She sulked that Will didn't love her and no longer paid her attention, but admitted she felt nothing for him. If her behavior toward Lord Bradbury had not cemented Holly's disliking for the girl, her views and treatment of Will certainly did.

Miss Flitter looked at something behind Holly's shoulder and straightened, her eyes lighting up. Holly looked behind her but only saw one of Grandfather's footman, a redheaded boy a bit younger than herself.

"If you'll excuse me." Miss Flitter left the drawing room.

Holly glanced outside. Great snowflakes continued to drift by, lazy and magical. The temptation to identify her ghost, human or otherwise, niggled at her. Her heart was quickly attaching itself to Will Berry. But first, she must resolve this

189

infatuation with the mystery man. Lord de Cadeau seemed convinced moonlight played a key role in ghostly appearances. However, with the present cloud cover, such an event tonight seemed impossible. Soon the moon would wane, and she would leave the castle and all opportunities to learn the truth. If only the clouds would part and let the moon through tonight! One more chance. All she wanted was one more chance.

Regardless, if her ghost never again showed himself, she would resolve to forget him forevermore.

Will joined her on the window seat. "What was that all about, if you don't mind my asking?"

Holly gave a start. Did he suspect she had been obsessing about her ghost again? "What?"

He tilted his chin toward the doorway through which Miss Flitter had disappeared. "Miss Flitter."

"Oh, that. Trying to ensure she is not brokenhearted."

"I think not." He gave a small, disbelieving chuckle.

"No, I agree." Emboldened by his attention, she said, "I enjoyed making music with you."

A soft light entered his eyes. "As did I. I hope you might be comfortable calling me Will."

Softly, she uttered the name she'd already started using for him in her thoughts. "Will."

"I like the sound of your angelic voice saying my name." His eyes caressed her face.

"I like it, too. Please call me Holly."

"Holly."

She shivered at the delicious sound.

"You are remarkably beautiful, Holly."

She should have looked down demurely, but couldn't tear her gaze from his. "Am I?"

"Do you not know?"

She swallowed and admitted in a flash of unusual boldness, "I don't think I ever cared so much about a gentleman's opinion as I care for yours."

"You are a rare bright spot of joy."

Her heart filled with light. "You are kind and thoughtful and intriguing."

He sat back, but let his hand brush against hers again.

She glanced around to see if anyone noticed. Her father watched them, intently. Oh dear. She folded her hands over her lap lest he recant his permission for Will to court her.

Joseph and Ivy stood together. "The hour is growing late and we are going to retire now. Good night, all."

Grandfather's head came up. "Good night." He gathered himself and, leaning on his cane, pushed himself slowly to his feet. He made a loose wave. "Sleep well."

All the guests stood, calling out goodnights.

Holly glanced regretfully at Will. Going to bed meant they must part. "Tomorrow, shall we go to St. Nicholas' church to take down the decorations?"

"I had hoped to do just that. It would give me an opportunity to speak with you of something important." With a tender expression, he added, "Holly."

What did he wish to say? "Perhaps you could walk with me to the stairs and tell me tonight?"

"It can wait until morning." His enigmatic expression stirred her imagination.

At the doorway, Ivy stopped and looked up. In exaggerated tones, Ivy said, "Oh dear. There is a nearly untouched kissing ball. We must remedy this at once." She and Joseph kissed under the ball of mistletoe, ivy, and spices decorated with a red ribbon.

Memories of her own kiss burst into Holly's mind. Her face burned and she looked away. Could everyone see her blush? Did they guess the reason?

"Come now," Joseph called merrily. "Let us all enjoy a kiss and pluck a berry." He tugged off a berry and held it up as a trophy.

Joseph's sister, Mary, and her husband followed suit. They parted grinning. Papa tugged on Mama, until she relented. Under the kissing ball, Papa kissed her thoroughly until she pulled away, giggling and smoothing her hair. Leave it to Papa to reduce Mama to a giggling girl despite her usual aplomb.

Mary pulled Grandfather beneath the kissing ball and planted a kiss on his wizened cheek. Holly hurried to him and kissed his other cheek. Grandfather chuckled and playfully batted them away.

After each couple had kissed, everyone turned expectantly to Holly and Will. Mama opened her mouth to speak, but Papa spoke into her ear. She turned away and strode into the great hall.

Will glanced at Holly with vulnerability, almost fear, in his eyes. He'd claimed to have a rather wild youth, but had he exaggerated? Perhaps he had little experience in truth and worried he might not do a proper job.

Or worse, he remembered her confession and was loath to kiss a girl who had willingly subjected herself to a stranger's kiss. But if that were the case, surely he would not have shown her such preference or received permission to court her, even going against her mother's wishes.

"Come now, don't be shy," Ivy called. "It's tradition."

The others called out encouragements.

Apology edged into Will's uncertain expression. "Do you mind?"

Holly's palms grew sweaty inside her gloves, and

her smile probably came out wobbly. "Who are we to go against tradition?" Did she sound desperate in her desire to kiss him?

Will held out a hand. She placed hers in it and walked at his side to the kissing ball. They stood, hand in hand, facing each other. His neck cloth shifted as he swallowed. He leaned in. Her heart stumbled and her knees shook. She closed her eyes. Aching, she lifted her face. His wassail-spiced breath warmed her mouth.

He kissed her cheek.

Stunned, she opened her eyes. The watching guests groaned and some chuckled.

"No, no, that won't do at all," Joseph's voice rang out. "Give her a proper kiss, Will."

Will froze. That intensity she occasionally saw in him returned. "Holly," he whispered. He swallowed again but instead of nervousness, a hunger that sent a flurry of shivers through her overtook his expression. "May I?"

She nodded. It didn't matter if he saw how much she wanted this, wanted him. Let him know. Let the whole world know.

He touched her chin, lifted it, and leaned in. Again, she closed her eyes. This time his lips touched hers, pliant and unbelievably gentle. Heat exploded at the contact and shot through her all the way down to

194

her tingling toes. Different from her mystery kiss, this one sang of affection and respect and a deep longing to be accepted. Sweeter, more chaste, more filled with caring, Will's kiss brought her a level of joy she'd never known. All the world faded away, leaving Will and the power of his affection, his touch, his kiss. Every moment of her life was designed to bring her to this single, perfect moment of bliss and wholeness.

"Ahem." Papa cleared his throat conspicuously.

Will pulled away all too quickly. A sound of distress caught in Holly's throat. It was over too soon. But oh, what a glorious kiss!

Holly opened her eyes. Will searched her expression, his earlier vulnerability returning. She poured all her happiness and affection into her smile. She wanted to stretch like a cat and revel in the delicious heat spiraling through her. Spectre or living man who refused to come forward, the conservatory encounter faded into meaningless noise. She'd been foolish to believe it had meant anything. Perhaps all kisses were as desirable. Surely that was the case or not so many people would share—or steal—them. But experiencing such a moment with Will, who clearly cared for her, and who she had grown so quickly to adore, lifted it up to the realm of heaven.

Their onlookers chuckled and a few applauded. Holly stepped back, her blush burning her face and neck. How could she have forgotten they had an audience?

Grinning, Will picked a berry off the mistletoe and took a brief, playful bow to the onlookers. The group dispersed.

Will smiled with such tenderness and joy that she almost burst into tears. All her life she'd been groomed to marry a lord and manage a household. She'd never dared hope she might find a man who would look at her with such complete acceptance and—dare she think it?—love. But the transcendent power of his kiss superseded the occurrence in the conservatory. Perhaps it didn't matter who it had been.

He took her hand. "Walk with me to the church after breakfast?"

"I look forward to it."

He kissed the back of her hand and stepped back, his eyes lowered.

Her bliss lasted until she reached her bedchamber where her mother stood waiting, her arms folded and her expression thunderous.

Holly halted. Her pulse drummed in her ears.

Mama said in a quiet voice of warning, "You will not throw yourself away on a mere vicar. I will not stand for it!"

Holly took a step back under the force of her mother's displeasure.

"That presumptuous Mr. Berry was much too familiar with you. Sitting so close at the pianoforte. Humph! *Kissing* you!"

Holly spread her hands and strove for a light tone. "Mama, it was just a mistletoe tradition."

"Mistletoe is for couples, and boys who want to kiss maids. Gentlemen ought never to use it to press their advantage, especially not on a young lady of a few days' acquaintance."

"He wasn't pressing his advantage. No one places any special meaning on mistletoe kisses." Holly would keep to herself how much it meant to her. Will seemed to place meaning on it as well.

"He clearly did, looking at you all cow-eyed. And you looked equally smitten. It was fortunate Lord Bradbury wasn't there to see it, or we would have lost all chance with him. Tomorrow, you will tell that vicar that his conduct this eve was appalling and that he is not to speak to you ever again."

All Holly's former tendencies to conform to her mother's will rose up and pulled on her. But if she did, she would never make another independent choice. She might even end up married to a title to please her mother, but not to a man who loved her. Her time to meekly accept had come to an end.

"Mama, Mr. Berry is—"

Mama took another step forward. "He is not for

197

you, do you hear me? I will not allow you to spend your time with the likes of him. You deserve better."

Anger gave Holly an added measure of courage. "Better? You mean of higher rank."

"Of course. I raised you to marry a lord, or at least a lord's heir such as Joseph is. Do not waste your upbringing on a nobody."

Every moment Holly had tried to be good, to do the right thing, wrestled with all the moments she'd trusted and obeyed her mother. She'd always equated obeying her parents with being good. But this time, what her mother asked of her was wrong. This time, obeying her mother paled against Holly's drive to hold fast to her integrity.

This was it then. This was Holly's time to take a stand, not for her beverage of choice, nor her favorite pastimes, nor how she styled her hair, but to secure her future happiness—true happiness with someone who loved her.

"You are treating him exactly the way everyone else treats you. I would think you, of all people, would be sympathetic to how that feels."

Mama's mouth dropped open.

Heedless, Holly continued, "I don't want someone of higher rank. I want *him*."

Mama sputtered. "Impossible!"

Holly plowed through. "He is a good and

honorable gentleman with a kind heart, and he makes me feel as if I am good enough just as I am, not as if I ought to always be on guard with everything I do and say, trying so hard to be perfect."

"Oh, Holly, don't be ridiculous."

"I know you checked Debrett's and learned he does, in fact, come from a respectable family. And as one of Joseph's oldest friends, he is not without connections. More importantly, I care for him and he cares for me. Even if he were a blacksmith, I'd feel the same way about him."

Her mother wagged a finger at her, her face reddening. "Young lady, you will do as I tell you or so help me—"

"Mama, please." Holly tried to keep a conciliatory tone. "I know your feelings, and how badly you want to impress everyone and fit in with the *beau monde*, and I'm sorry his profession displeases you, but I must follow my heart. Papa gave his permission. I have already made my choice."

Her mother went very still and the most sorrowful expression Holly had ever seen appeared. "You never used to be so willful. I had such high hopes for you. Now I will forever face the same insults that have dogged me all my life. And so will you." She strode out.

Trembling, Holly sank onto the bed. She had

achieved her goal of gaining a measure of independence, at least, enough to choose her suitor. But at what cost? In her desire to gain her independence, she'd almost forgotten how badly her mother wanted to protect Holly from the cuts so many sticklers of society had doled out all her life. Long ago, Holly had promised she would marry well so as to protect her mother and the rest of her family. She had broken that promise, and hurt her mother.

And worse, what if her relationship with Will fell short? He might change his mind. He hadn't exactly asked her to marry him. After courting, they might find that they did not suit after all. If so, she would have alienated her mother for nothing.

If she and Will married, would she always be torn between two worlds?

Chapter Fourteen

Will turned over in bed, reliving Holly's kiss. He had tried to keep the kiss more chaste than the one he'd given her as the "ghost" lest she know the truth right then. Besides, they'd had a decided lack of privacy. Their first kiss, the one he had intended to give to Phoebe, had been meant to demonstrate his skill as well as elicit a passionate response. The mistletoe kiss had been meant exclusively for Holly, to show her how much she had come to mean to him. Afterwards, she'd looked as dazzled as he'd felt, with no signs of suspicion or recognition.

His head filled with fanciful plans to marry Holly and have a houseful of children with whom they would share laughter, music, and Christmas traditions.

Of course, Holly might be so angry when he finally confessed his deception that she would refuse to see him again. The very real fear of losing her now turned him cold.

Will gave up on sleep and arose. All lay still and quiet. Not even the servants moved about. The fire had burned out in the hearth, abandoning the room to face a winter's chill unprotected. In the cold room, he donned a banyan and added a log.

He rehearsed words to tell her the truth. What could he say that would not make her feel used—not make it seem a mistake? Every explanation he tested sounded more sordid than the last. She would probably be furious. She had every reason. Would she hate him?

Would she be hurt?

Eventually, the servants awoke, their stirrings heralding that time he must face her with the truth. A maid tiptoed in to add to the fire.

Faint grey light seeped in from the windows. Will threw open one of the draperies and peered through the frosty window. Outside, a blanket of white coated the world. More snow swirled by. They ought not visit the church today to take down the Christmas decorations. Perhaps this church, like many homes, left the decorations up until Twelfth Night. He should have thought to ask.

Somehow, he must get Holly alone and confess. He'd deceived her long enough and it was time to face the consequences. Waiting longer would only make it worse. Dread stayed with him as he shaved and dressed.

As he went down to breakfast, Joseph called him. "Sleep well last night, Will?"

Will turned. "Good morning."

Joseph wore a smug expression. "Not a wink, eh? Too busy reliving kissing my sister-in-law?"

Will let out a scoffing noise. "You and your wife conspired against me."

"We conspired *for* you. There's a difference. It's clear how you feel about each other. Ivy and I just thought we'd help it along. You are planning to court her, aren't you?"

He nodded. "Of course—now that I have her father's permission." Although, that permission might be a moot point if she told her father that she refused to be courted by cads who stole kisses and then lied.

Joseph wagged a finger at Will, his eyes twinkling. "Shrewd strategy going to the father."

Will smiled at Joseph's attempt to give Will all the credit to following Joseph's idea in the first place.

His friend continued, "I'm happy to know you haven't changed that much from our college days."

Will gulped. "I hope I have changed a great deal. But not as much as I thought."

Joseph clapped him on the shoulder. "A misspent youth doesn't condemn you to the life of a sinner. You of all people ought to know that. If a vicar doesn't believe in repentance, what hope is there for any of us?"

"I hope everyone feels that way." Perhaps if he could somehow demonstrate how sorry he was for kissing Holly by mistake, and for not apologizing on the spot, she would be more likely to forgive him.

Of course, he wasn't truly sorry about the kiss. But he could genuinely apologize for the way he went about it and for any distress it caused her.

Joseph peered into his face. "You're thinking much too hard about this. Come into the breakfast room. You always think better on a full stomach."

With his stomach already filled—with bricks— Will doubted he could eat. "I need to speak to Miss Gray alone. Do you have any suggestions?"

"Hmmm. Ivy and I could show the two of you the gallery and then accidentally leave you alone for a few minutes."

Will nodded. "I would appreciate it."

Joseph paused. "You will be a gentleman with my sister-in-law, won't you?"

Will couldn't blame Joseph for the question; they had known each other too long. Still, the idea that Joseph doubted his intentions deepened Will's regret for his misspent youth. "I vow it."

Joseph nodded. "Then leave it to me."

Will entered the breakfast room at Joseph's side. The other guests, including Lord Bradbury, were already at the table. Some chatted, others read the newspaper. Mrs. Gray was noticeably absent. Holly sat at one end of the table, thoughtfully pouring chocolate into her cup.

He sat next to her and affected a tone of exaggerated horror. "You like that nasty stuff?"

Holly looked up and smiled. "I do. So much better than tea."

"Dreadful." He grinned.

She smiled. Something about her seemed subdued but resolute. Did she regret the mistletoe kiss? Beneath the table, she slid her hand over to his and gave it a squeeze. A bold move made with confidence. The softness in her eyes returned—the same expression that had been there after their mistletoe kiss. Dare he hope she'd continue to look at him like that after he told her the truth?

"I like coffee best," he confessed. "I suppose there's no harm in having two pots of our favorite drink."

Her hand holding the silver pitcher froze. "Two pots?"

Will bit his lip. His statement had been wildly presumptive. He hadn't even begun a formal courtship, much less asked her to marry him. And he still had to get through his confession. That might put a halt to all his plans. Would she truly be so angry that she'd refuse to allow him to court her?

How could he salvage the foolish statement about having two pots? He chose a teasing tone. "Er, yes. Two or even three pots of hot beverages seem to be common for big gatherings." He gestured to the pots down the center of the table. "Chocolate for those of you irrational people who like that vile stuff." He almost laughed at her playfully outraged expression. "Coffee for real men like me, and tea for everyone else who conforms to fashion. We could even request that wassail be served every morning, too."

"Real men like coffee, hmmm? I might need more convincing of that statement."

"I have a few ideas." He grinned.

A coy light glinted in her eyes and a husky tone caressed her voice. "I am willing to entertain your suggestions." She sipped her chocolate and closed her eyes. "Heavenly." She opened her eyes. "You truly don't mind that I don't enjoy your drink of choice?"

"You can enjoy whatever your heart desires, love."

Did she smile at his term of endearment, or his statement? After his confession, she might never smile at him again.

He poured a cup of coffee and helped himself to a scone but could hardly eat a bite. How would he tell her?

"Do you have a preference for how I wear my

hair?" She touched her hair pulled back into a low knot.

Her question took him aback. "Er, no. The way you usually wear it with all the curls is nice, especially for formal occasions. This way," he gestured to her hair, "is just as pretty. I'd love to see it down, sometime."

She seemed to consider. "My mother is of the opinion that ladies in the marriage mart ought to wear their hair a certain way or they risk hampering their chances."

Her mother had very strong opinions to the point of being domineering. Had she been hard on Holly last night? The thought of Holly facing down her dragon of a mother raised protective instincts in him.

Under the cover of the table, he squeezed her hand. "Perhaps some people would agree. I am less hard to please, I suppose. Hairstyles are not a necessary side dish for the marriage café, at least, not on my menu."

Her thoughtfulness lifted, and her tender expression wrapped him in softness. Then she smiled, probably at his echo of her own amusing words about the marriage café, just as he had hoped. She intertwined her fingers with his and a sensual gesture that sent his imagination to new heights.

"You need not go to effort to please me," he said.

"You are already a remarkable lady. I have never met anyone as kind and genuine and truly lovely in every regard."

Instead of blushing or looking demure, she smiled even more broadly. An expression he could only identify as happiness overcame her. "And you are a remarkable gentleman. I have never met anyone as thoughtful and considerate and truly fine in every regard. I feel I *can* be genuine with you, not try to fit some ideal."

"I hope you never change."

She did look down then, but without any signs of playing coy. If only he could hold onto this comfortable, familiar sensation. But with such a lie as what happened in the conservatory between them, it would never be real.

"And I hope your opinion of me never changes." He gently squeezed her hand as he reached down inside and gathered his courage. With her gaze once again fixed upon him, he nodded to the windows where large flakes fluttered past. "I suspect the snow is too deep for a trip to the church today. However, Joseph and Ivy offered to show us their gallery. It is impressive. Would you care to view it with me? We could converse there, as well." He added the last bit in case she didn't catch on to his hope of speaking with her in private.

Christmas Secrets

"Lovely." That fond smile may not appear any more. Ever. That same sensation of being kicked in the gut hit him so hard he nearly doubled over.

Joseph and his missus approached them, both with mischievous grins. They obviously expected Will to propose, or at least steal a kiss, in the gallery—not expose his lie.

"Today is Boxing Day," Mrs. Chestnut said, "everyone is invited to help us prepare the boxes in about an hour. But first, we would very much like to show you both the gallery. Would now be convenient?"

A drum roll sounded in Will's head. Heaven help him. "Of course." He stood and offered a hand to Holly.

While the others chatted as they walked up the main staircase to the gallery, Will ran through possible explanations, each sounding more cowardly and boorish than the last. How could he explain?

They reached their destination. The red walls set off the family coat of arms and dozens of paintings from floor to ceiling. Will hardly saw them. His throat tightened, and perspiration ran down his back, despite the cold room.

"Oh, dear," Ivy said. "It's so cold in here. We should have instructed the servants to build a fire. I think I'll fetch a shawl."

"I'll accompany you, my sweet," Joseph said. He quirked a brow as he turned to Will and Holly. "You two don't mind, do you? We'll return momentarily."

Will gave a loose wave when he couldn't manage a reply. Hot and cold chills ran down his limbs.

"Are you well?" Holly asked.

Will made an inarticulate sound.

"You've been very distracted." Did he imagine fear in her voice? "Do...do you regret kissing me under the mistletoe?"

Will pushed aside his concern for his own interests and took a good look at her. Her earlier playful mood faded. Fear and uncertainty dimmed the light in her eyes.

He touched her arm. "No, of course not. Last night's kiss was magical. I don't regret it."

Her brows continued to draw together. "Then what is it?"

This was it. Now was the time. Courage. "Holly, I have grown to care very deeply for you. And I have something to tell you that I fear will cause you to lose your good opinion of me."

"I doubt that very much. Come, let's sit." She gestured to a round scarlet chair and lowered onto it. "What is it?"

He sank into the cushions. "I believe I mentioned to you that I had a rather wild youth."

"You did."

"And since taking my position, I have made every attempt to put that wildness behind me and to live the way a vicar ought. The way a gentleman of honor ought." He paused.

She slid both of her small hands around one of his. He gripped them and offered up a silent plea that it would not be the last time she willingly touched him.

He clawed at his courage. "As you know, for several days I courted Miss Flitter. Or at least I thought that is what we were doing. She, as you know, viewed me as a vaguely interesting diversion until someone of higher rank came along."

"She used you most shamefully."

"I am not blameless, as you will soon see." He tried to draw in a breath but the air thickened, too heavy to breathe. "I don't know how to say this."

"You can tell me." She looked so trusting.

He pressed forward like a soldier to a doomed battle. "I am ashamed to say, that in the course of our supposed courtship, I kissed her. It was unremarkable, due, I assumed, to her innocence." He didn't dare look at Holly. Surely, she'd be disappointed. Gads, but speaking of such delicate matters to a lady—a lady whose opinion mattered more than anything—proved more difficult than facing his strictest schoolmaster to own up to his latest prank and its subsequent punishment.

"She told me later that she was not as inexperienced as I supposed. It seems our kiss was unremarkable because we had no true affection between us. Anyway, at the time, I thought I needed to know her better." He rubbed sweaty palms down his thighs and finally snuck a glance.

Only a thoughtful, watchful stare came his way.

"I thought perhaps she..." he stalled out. It seemed crass to say he thought she needed more practice to make kissing more pleasant or if he kissed her more passionately that she would warm up. "I thought to test whether her feelings about me were in earnest so I invited her to meet me so we could kiss again."

Holly's inevitable disappointment arrived.

He tried to moisten his lips but his mouth had gone as dry as old parchment. "Because she and I have both spent other Christmases here with Joseph and his grandfather, and were aware of their tradition of telling ghost stories, we agreed to meet in the conservatory under the pretense of looking for ghosts. Or at least, I thought she had agreed."

Understanding dawned in her eyes. "It was you?"

He nodded and tried to swallow but his cravat seemed bent on strangling him.

She slid her hands out of his and stood. "You kissed me, thinking you were kissing *her*?"

He leaped to his feet, partly out of habit to stand when a lady stood, and partly to stay closer to her. "I did. I'm sorry."

Hurt filled her expressive eyes. Her mouth worked and the color drained out of her face.

Cold arrows shot through him. Anger, he'd expected, but not hurt. What had he done? He took her hand. "Please understand. When kissing you was so much more...remarkable, wonderful, amazing...than kissing her had been, I knew the girl I was kissing in the conservatory could not possibly have been Phoebe Flitter."

Her hand remained limp in his. Faintly, she said. "It was a mistake."

"It was—but I cannot regret it. It opened my eyes. I noticed you, really noticed you, for the first time. I also started paying better attention to her, to how little she suited me and how little she cared for me, and I for her."

Holly withdrew her hand, turned, and took a few steps away. "When you first realized it was me and not her, why didn't you tell me?"

"I panicked. I was so ashamed that I'd mistreated you, and guilt-ridden that I had cheated on Phoebe. I am sorry. I should have revealed myself instead of leaving."

"You told me it was a ghost." She turned, her accusing, wounded expression piercing him like nails through his flesh. "You almost had me convinced of the possibility."

"I didn't want you to think it was anyone else, especially Bradbury—at first because I was trying to protect you. I didn't want your expectations toward him raised. You would be hurt if he didn't come up to snuff. I was also trying to be fair to him. Later, I didn't want to give him the credit for a kiss you confessed that you enjoyed."

Her breath came in short, noisy spurts. "You deceived me."

Her words slashed at Will like a blade. He fought to remain upright instead of folding in half. "I did. It was ungentlemanly and dishonest and cowardly. All I can do is tell you how sorry I am that I caused you grief."

"Sorry." She let out a scoffing noise. "Sorry. Yes, I'm sorry, too. I'm sorry everything I thought we had was built on a lie. And now I have earned my mother's hatred for...for nothing. I should have listened to her."

She shuddered in a breath. Hugging herself, she looked at him one final time with all the hurt and fear of a lost child. She turned and strode toward the door.

"Holly," he called. He hurried after her. As he

caught up to her, he grasped her arm gently. "Holly, please."

"Don't." Her mouth worked, and her eyes brightened with tears. Tears! She shrugged out of his grasp and ran from the room.

Will collapsed onto the nearest chair. He ground his palms into his eye sockets. All his worst fears hit him full force. He had been a lying scoundrel. He had no one to blame but himself for losing a remarkable lady, a lady he clearly did not deserve.

Chapter Fifteen

Exhausted from weeping, Holly sat with her forehead resting on the window of her bedchamber. The snow had stopped falling, leaving the gloom of an overcast winter's day. Downstairs, festivities carried on, and occasionally children's voices and laughter carried up to her. Normally, Holly would revel in the Boxing Day activities, but today her wounded heart bled out all her joy.

Her toe-curling kiss in the conservatory had been meant for another.

A mistake.

Her relationship with Will, all he'd done, all he'd said, had been a fallacy. He had only pursued her out of an obligation to do his duty by her. Or perhaps she'd been a convenient second choice when his relationship with Phoebe had failed.

What kind of man arranges assignations, then kisses whatever girl happens to be there? Then, instead of owning up to his actions, lies to cover up his mistakes, making up wild stories about kissing ghosts? She could not love such a man. How could a vicar, of all people, behave in such a way?

On more than one occasion he had admitted to his misspent youth, but she'd assumed he'd changed. Apparently, he had not changed so much.

Now Holly was alone, rejected by her mother, and with only the tarnished memories of two perfect kisses based on a lie.

The bounder! Her heartache faded to anger. He'd used her and lied to her. She'd been a foolish, naïve little schoolgirl to fall for his charm. She should have slapped him. The problem was she couldn't picture herself striking him, even though he deserved it.

She got up and paced to the hearth and back. If only she had listened to her mother and ignored her attraction to Will, focusing instead on Lord Bradbury. He would never have done such an underhanded thing.

Again, that sensation of being trapped between two worlds overwhelmed her. She may never repair her relationship with her mother, nor did she wish to blindly obey her every decree. But Mama always seemed to know what to do, and Holly missed her confident counsel. True, her mother could be overbearing, but she was also wise and had guided Holly through many difficulties as she grew up.

Perhaps it wasn't too late to renew her determination to encourage Lord Bradbury. Yet to be bound to such a stiff, formal man, always worried about behaving exactly as she ought...

Holly had to escape this room, but could not bear the gathering downstairs. After washing her face, she donned her heaviest clothes, went downstairs, and slipped out a side door to the wintry gardens.

The snow on the walkways made soft crunches as she marched under barren flocked trees and past snowy shrubs forming severe geometric shapes. Frozen ponds and still fountains sat lifeless. Empty. Bleak. Holly strode, hardly seeing her surroundings, to the far edge of the gardens.

What to do now? How to heal her heart wounded by a callous, lying rake? Perhaps rake was too strong a word, but still. She refused to spend the rest of her life in misery over such a man. Mama had been right about him.

How to make amends with her mother without losing a measure of her independence? Holly would no longer meekly adjust every hair to meet her mother's approval, but she still needed Mama's guidance if she had any way of regaining it without losing herself.

The garden path led Holly to less sculpted areas that eventually gave way to a wilderness section of the grounds. She stared out over the white, sterile landscape that concealed all signs of life. The lure to keep walking called to her, but she had no wish to get lost. She followed the path back toward the main part of the castle. Her toes numbed but she was loath to return to the group.

"Holly." Her father's voice glided to her on the freezing air. "Out here alone?"

"I needed the solitude." She waited until he caught up to her and they fell in step.

"Cold today."

She nodded.

"You and Will Berry make a nice couple."

She let out a scoffing noise. Her heart squeezed and her tear ducts burned.

"What has happened?"

"He..." she swallowed. "I have decided we would not suit."

"The kiss suggested otherwise."

She closed her eyes but it didn't help. Memories of the mistletoe kiss, and how it had rivaled, possibly exceeded, the beauty of the conservatory kiss, rushed in and unfolded before her mind's eye, along with all the delicious sensations of affection and warmth and belonging. All false.

"I found out something about him."

Papa waited.

She huffed, her breath making great clouds. "He wasn't completely honest with me about it. Not an outright lie, but close."

It was an understatement, but she didn't dare tell

her father the whole truth. Will didn't deserve to lose his position. Besides, having to choose between a long-time friend and the family into which he had married would put Joseph in an awkward position. Moreover, if word got out, her own reputation might be called into question as well.

Papa nodded. "A lie of omission."

"Yes, I suppose you could call it that."

Her father said thoughtfully, "Sometimes good men make bad choices."

Well, true, but this was an exceedingly bad choice.

They walked for several minutes, neither speaking. Time in Papa's presence always soothed her, with no pressure to walk or speak or dress a certain way. He said little, but what he said always carried such weight, such wisdom.

He spoke again. "Difficult to confess one's weaknesses, mistakes. The more you love, the more his or her opinion matters. You stand to lose more."

Holly absorbed that. "So, the more he came to care for me, the more difficult it was to tell me the whole truth because he feared I would reject him."

Papa nodded. "Human nature."

Holly had probably reacted exactly the way Will had feared. But she'd been justified. He'd kept the truth a secret and led her down a path of deceit, feeding that ridiculous idea that she'd been kissed by a ghost.

In an uncharacteristically conversational mood, Papa continued, "Half-truths and omissions that seem harmless at the time often become important later."

Will had said that he wanted to protect her from expecting a proposal from Lord Bradbury, and so she wouldn't suspect anyone else. An honorable motive. And she had suggested the ghost in the first place; he'd only encouraged that belief.

"You've given me much to consider, Papa."

They reached the inner garden closest to the terrace.

He gestured. "Coming in?"

"Not just yet. You go ahead."

"Don't be long."

She nodded. As Papa strode away, Holly took another path that led to the east side of the castle. Voices and laughter reached her. She was missing all the fun. But she just couldn't face all that holiday cheer.

She reviewed her father's words. Perhaps she had misjudged Will. Still, the truth remained that her first kiss had been a mistake. That alone hurt more than all of it. And, to make matters worse, her second kiss had been somewhat coerced by everyone taking turns beneath the mistletoe. Had he been so hesitant because he feared she'd know him by his kiss?

Did she dare trust him? If he deceived her once, he might do it again. She missed him already, and they'd only spent the afternoon apart. Did she dare give him another chance? Papa seemed convinced she should. But he didn't know the whole story.

Will had accidentally kissed her when he meant to kiss another. It was the worst form of rejection. Then he'd run away like a coward. To compound matters, he'd deceived her, which was as bad as a lie. He'd had ample opportunity to tell her the truth. He had been wrong not to do so. Not telling her made his original transgression—his original rejection—so much worse.

On and on she walked until she could no longer feel her feet. Her legs ached and her body shook. She turned back. Her solitude must continue inside, it seemed.

"Holly." That silky baritone could only be Will's.

She lifted her head. He strode toward her. She'd almost forgotten how dear his face had become. His sober expression and entreating eyes brushed against her resolve to be angry with him. Snowflakes, smaller than before, fell with a determination to reach the ground at high speed. Equally determined, Will moved to her heedless of the weather. Snow clung to the hem of his greatcoat and coated his boots so thickly that they appeared white instead of black. His nose and cheeks were as red as apples. How long had he been out in the cold?

She waited for him, tempted to run away but her frozen feet refused to move. Or perhaps her aching but still foolishly hopeful heart had taken command.

A desperate sort of pleading flowed out of him in a tangible current. Regret and pain darkened his eyes. He stopped in front of her.

His expression shifted to that of concern. "Your lips are blue and your chin is quivering." He unbuttoned his greatcoat and threw it over her shoulders. After fastening the top button under her chin, he held out a hand. "You need to get inside and warm yourself."

The wounded animal inside her wanted to push him away, reject his aid, lash out at him. But she lacked the strength. Sadness had drained away all her fight. She ignored his hand but moved unresisting toward the castle.

His voice rumbled. "I never meant to hurt you."

"You did hurt me." Her voice quivered and her eyes burned. "In many ways."

How could he have kissed her like that, intending it for a silly, conniving little tart like Phoebe Flitter? Pain struck at her again, cutting through her numbness.

He said nothing for a long moment. "I'm sorry. I

hope you will forgive me. Someday." The last word came out hoarse.

She glanced up at him. His jaw clenched and his lips pressed together. His breath came out in puffs. She ought to give him another chance, but her pain and fatigue made it difficult to sort her feelings. Just because he looked sorrowful and gave her his coat didn't mean he deserved complete forgiveness.

She trudged at his side, silent, grim, aching. She glanced at him again. The wounded hopelessness in his expression chipped at her pride. Did he truly deserve to suffer? How she missed the laughter in his eyes, the contagious grin, the spring in his step. Her father's words came back to her: *Sometimes good men make bad choices.* She had also made plenty of bad choices.

She tried for a measure of peace between them. "Thank you for your coat."

He nodded.

"Are you cold?"

He shrugged.

They reached a side door and he held it open for her. She stumbled inside on numb feet and legs. Inside, he led her to the library where they found Grandfather dozing next to a roaring fire.

Will guided her forward. "My lord, may Miss Gray sit next to you? I fear she spent too much time outside."

Grandfather roused. "Of course, young Will. Come here, sweeting." He gestured to a second armchair drawn next to the fire opposite him.

Will led her to the heat. She tripped over her own feet. Will put a steadying hand beneath each elbow and tugged on her until she managed to reach the fireplace. Standing in front of the chair, she fumbled with her gloves and buttons but had no feeling in her hands. Will tore off his gloves, and removed hers, before removing his coat and then hers from around her shoulders. He laid her coat over a nearby chair.

In long strides, Will left. His absence opened up a new ache inside. She should not have been so cold to him.

She sank to the chair but could hardly feel the blaze in the hearth. The fire popped and crackled, the scent of wood and cloves and cinnamon filling the air. On the mantle, an ornately gilded clock ticked. Below the face, a couple dressed in the frilly clothes of the previous era leaned toward one another as if about to share a kiss, forever frozen in expectancy of an event that would never happen.

"Good lad, that Will Berry," Grandfather said.

Holly tried to give him a smile.

"I watched him grow up. Full of mischief that one, always testing his limits and questioning the rules. So full of life. He found humor and joy in everything. He's steady now and tries hard to do what's expected of him." He nodded. "I hope you and he will be happy." The fondness in Grandfather's wrinkled expression faced off with her own conflicted feelings for Will.

Holly could not find words to say in response.

"Trouble between you two?"

The butler entered carrying a tray with a china pot that the family only used for chocolate. "Mr. Berry ordered chocolate for Miss Gray," the butler intoned. "Fortunately, cook had some she was keeping warm."

Holly blinked. "He asked you to bring me chocolate?"

"Yes, miss. He seemed most concerned you'd caught a chill." He set the chocolate on a little round table next to her chair, and placed another pot next to Grandfather. "I brought you some more tea, my lord. Will you be needing anything else?"

"Perhaps you ought to send for Miss Gray's maid," Lord de Cadeau said. "She looks as if she could use a hot bath and a change into some dry clothes."

"Mr. Berry already made that request, my lord. The maids are filling a bath now."

Will had thoughtfully seen to her needs, even after she'd been so curt with him. He was a good man. And even good men sometimes made mistakes. But mostly, they were kind, thoughtful, and generous.

Had she pushed him too far away?

Chapter Sixteen

Will glared out of the window at the falling snow. It would be just his luck that the weather would obliterate his apology. Perhaps it had been a stupid way to apologize, anyway. Besides, it was probably pointless to try. Holly was right. He'd been selfish and unfeeling. She had every reason to be angry. He didn't deserve her forgiveness. He glared at his spectacles sitting benignly on his bedside table. Until recently, they helped him rein in his baser nature. Until his baser nature had proven too powerful.

After changing into dry clothing and warming himself, he paced back and forth in his bedchambers. He missed her. He missed her comforting acceptance, her beautiful voice, her perpetual cheer.

He refused to give up. He could do better. *Be* better. It might be a lost cause, but he had to try.

How did one apologize to a woman? A lady. A lady who had every right to be furious but instead was hurt. His elder brothers had used flowers as a way of worming their way back into a lady's good graces. But that seemed a trite gesture. And this time of year, flowers of that kind would be difficult to find. Besides, he had not only angered her; he'd hurt her. She'd looked at him like an abandoned child. Her stark pain, which he had inflicted on her, battered him until he felt ragged and raw. No apology seemed acceptable. She'd been so overset that she had spent far too much time out in the cold. Had she caught a chill?

He opened the door and hailed a passing maid. "Please learn if Miss Gray is well, and where she is at present."

The maid bobbed a curtsy and entered the servants' stairs.

Will turned back and dragged a hand through his hair. How could he reach Holly?

Did he deserve a second chance?

Sunlight painted bright squares on the floor of his bedchamber. Sunlight? Outside, the late afternoon sun had split the clouds. Perhaps he could try again with his apology. It might be foolish, and surely insufficient, but he had to do something.

He put on the boots he'd worn earlier that day. No need to get two pairs wet. After wrapping up in his scarf, he donned his overcoat. He paused, and buried his face in the cloth. Holly's subtle scent still clung to the wool.

A scratch at his door caught his attention. "Come," he called.

The maid peered in. "Miss Gray's lady's maid said she is well and will be at dinner, sir."

"Thank you." He handed her a coin for her trouble and headed downstairs.

Outside, he found the area that would be visible from her window where he'd left his previous message. The new layer of snow had covered most of the words, leaving only faint indentations behind. Using the same path he'd trod earlier in the morning, Will stamped down the snow to reform his message. Cold and wet, he stood back to survey his work.

It was stupid. Perhaps he ought to seek Joseph's advice. Or his grandfather's. They might have better ideas how Will could redeem himself with her.

Chapter Seventeen

Warm and dry, her mind still spinning over Will, Holly sat at the pianoforte next to her sister as they played a favorite duet from their childhood. Ivy set the rhythm and led the duet. Holly played mindlessly, relying on her fingers' muscles to remember the part.

"Mama is angry at you, isn't she?" Ivy commented with amusement in her voice.

Holly glanced at her inquiringly.

Ivy's lips turned upward. "She was especially irritable when she helped me with all the boxes. And you vanished outside."

Holly let out her breath. "I disobeyed her."

"It must have been some show of defiance." Ivy sounded almost impressed.

"It has been a series of rebellions, each greater than the last."

"You surprise me," Ivy said. "You never used to have any sort of backbone regarding her."

"I had backbone. I just...I wanted to be good. To make her proud of me."

"I know. I envied that about you. Were you right?"

"About?"

"When you defied her. Were you right? Did you stand up for something important?"

"It was important to me."

Ivy nudged her with her elbow without breaking the rhythm. "Then don't let her feelings bother you. Sometimes one must hold one's ground."

"I know. But she won't even look at me."

They ended the song. Ivy started another one they knew just as well. Holly joined in the second measure.

Ivy bumped Holly with her elbow again. "Be of good cheer. She'll forgive you if you try to make an attempt. She makes a big show of anger, but she forgives just as easily if you appear penitent enough."

"But I'm not truly sorry."

"Not for what you did, which I am guessing was refusing to continue to encourage Lord Bradbury, and instead reveal your preference for Will. But you are sorry for being at odds with her, aren't you?"

"That is true."

"Have you tried to make amends?"

Holly missed a note. "Yes, this morning before breakfast I went to her room. She refused to see me."

"Try again. But first, tell me why you and Will are avoiding each other."

"We had a misunderstanding." More softly, Holly added, "He hurt my feelings."

"He did?" A protective tone entered Ivy's voice.

"In his defense, he didn't mean to. It was actually an honest mistake." A mistake. That is all his kiss had been. Hurt opened up all over again.

"Oh." She paused as if deciding whether to be angry at Will. "Did he apologize?"

Reluctantly, Holly admitted, "He did. Multiple times, in fact. And he truly looked sorry."

"And?"

"I am afraid I was quite unforgiving," Holly confessed.

"Then you have two people with whom you need to forge a repair."

Holly sighed.

"Love is about apologizing," Ivy said, "even when the other person is at fault. It's the relationship that matters, not whether or not you are right."

They played without conversing for the remainder of the song. Holly hadn't meant to be so stubborn, but she had been deeply wounded. She had also felt the need to protect herself against further rejection.

Despite his mistakes, Will Berry was still a good man with a big heart. Surely, he deserved another chance. But could she let go of her hurt feelings and wounded pride enough to forgive him?

"Thank you, Ivy. You've grown wise since your marriage."

Ivy's mouth quirked into a sly smile. "A little, perhaps. Now go talk to Mama. Then make things right with Will. He looked like a kicked puppy all day."

"Yes, ma'am." Holly shared a smile with her sister. She arose. "I'm going to change for dinner."

Holly went to her mother's bedchamber and found her alone. A quick, startled glance came her way. Mama sat stiffly on the edge of a settee near the fireplace.

Holly perched next to her mother. Softly, she said, "Mama, I love you." Her mother stared. At least she appeared to be listening.

Taking courage from Mama's lack of anger, she pushed on. "I have always trusted you. You are one of the wisest and strongest women I know." Holly took her hands and squeezed them. "I know that your goal to find a lord for me to marry is not only so you can improve your standing in society; you also have my best interests at heart. You want me to have doors open to me that you have not had most of your life. You want me to be happy and well cared for. I am sure you even want me to be loved. And you've done well with Ivy and Charles. They are both happy with the matches you made for them."

Mollified, Mama nodded. "Just so."

"I am making a choice based on my heart. It's not

the choice you would have made for me but I have found a fine gentleman who comes from a good family. He has respectable friends in Joseph and Lord de Cadeau. I hope you trust me and respect me enough to accept my choice. I want the freedom to decide for myself if he is the one I wish to marry."

"Why do you like him?" Mama finally asked.

"He's kind, and witty, and he has such a zest for life. He's well-mannered but not so obsessed with being proper that he's stuffy and inflexible. I am comfortable with him. I don't need to put on a show, or worry whether what I do or say is correct. He doesn't care what I like to drink or how I wear my hair or if I enjoy ice skating. He's thoughtful. He has a generous spirit."

Mama picked at a nearby cushion. "A vicar for a son-in-law is not someone about whom I would be so proud to write to my parents." She paused and her eyes unfocused. "I remember what it was like to be young and in love. I fell in love with the son of our steward. But I had vowed to marry a gentleman who came from a noble lineage."

Holly stared at her hands. She did not want to hear about how Mama married Papa for his social standing and not because she loved him.

"I grew to love your father, Holly."

Holly lifted her head.

"Because of that, I knew if you children married the right sort of people, not just nobility, but those with honor and principles, you could be happy. You might even find love."

Holly held her breath. Was Mother actually relenting?

Mama continued toying with the fringe on the cushion. "I suppose you could do a lot worse than a vicar. He certainly is handsome and charming. Vicars are considered respectable. I am sure I can focus on his family connections that are not so modest."

Had her mother just given her approval?

Mama looked her in the eye. "Do you love him?"

Holly hesitated. "I am not sure. I have never been in love. I want to be with him. When he is out of the room, I am lonely. I want to make him happy. It hurts me to see him sad."

"Love means putting others' happiness ahead of your own. It also means swallowing your pride more than once."

Holly was beginning to understand that all too well. "I know. I do want to do everything I can to make him smile and to bring him comfort and joy." She ached knowing she had hurt him, far worse than her own pain had been when she'd felt that he'd deceived and rejected her. "I think I do love him."

"Then promise me one thing."

"Anything, Mama."

"That you will be sure before you agree to marry him. Absolutely sure. No doubts. If you have even the tiniest doubt, insist on a longer courtship until you are sure. Or cry off."

Relief and joy turned Holly feather-light. She clasped her hands together. "Yes, Mama. I will."

"Very well." Mama patted her hand.

"Thank you, Mama." Despite her mother's views about embraces being a lack of decorum, Holly threw her arms around her.

Mama clucked and patted her. "There, there. No need for all that. You didn't think I'd disown you, did you?"

Holly's smile came out watery. "No, Mama."

Perhaps she need not give up her heart's desire after all. Her parents' approval, and certainly their love, did not depend on her choice of suitors.

She had one task yet: apologize to Will for being so harsh and judgmental. She'd been wallowing in self-pity, feeling so rejected, and perhaps even proud, that she hadn't noticed how her response to his confession must have hurt him. It had surely taken a great deal of courage to tell her what he'd done. Instead of understanding, *she* had rejected *him*.

It was time to make that right. And she would. Her reconciliation with her mother gave her courage.

Lighter of heart, she danced into her room. As she rang for her maid, she glanced outside. A figure stamped through the snow. Was that Will? She moved to the window and watched as he tramped out a message tracing a faded one the earlier snowfall had dusted, making it hard to read. The new, freshly tromped message read:

I'm sorry. Please forgive me.

With most heart-felt regrets,

Your ghost

She didn't know whether to laugh at the sentiment and the way he'd delivered it, or weep for the effort he'd put into his apology. Her anger and bitterness toward him tasted sour in her mouth. How could she have been angry with such a sweet gentleman?

He must have composed the first message this afternoon before coming to find her, giving her his coat, and bringing her inside to get warm. Then he'd returned to leave her the message again so she'd be sure to see it. How like him to be so thoughtful!

After dinner, she would eat a generous slice of humble pie and hope it was enough to make amends.

Chapter Eighteen

Cold and discouraged, Will tromped inside his bedchamber. His foolish message probably would only puzzle others, and Holly might not even see it. He let out a hopeless breath. Everything he thought of doing to show his regret would be wholly inadequate.

The footman Joseph had assigned to act as his valet met him in his bedchamber, frantic that Will had come in late and left little time to dress for dinner. Dinner. Where he'd see Holly. Would she even look at him? Now that he'd finally gained permission to court her, she was more untouchable than ever. And it was his fault.

The harried valet had Will warmed and dressed in record time. Heavy of heart, Will opened the door to his bedchamber and stepped into the corridor. A crackle sounded from below. He lifted his foot. A folded paper laid on the floor.

Inside, he read:

Mr. B,

Please meet me in the conservatory after dinner.

No signature. But the script was decidedly

feminine. Dare he hope Holly had written it? She might only wish to tell him all the reasons she never wanted to see him again, but his pitifully optimistic heart ventured to hope she was willing to give him another chance.

Or it could be her mother who planned to drive a stake through his chest.

Either way, he would face the consequences and come what may.

If Holly had told her parents what he had done, they might very well report his actions. His reputation would be damaged. He could lose his position, which would ruin his career. He would disappoint his parents. If any scandal arose from it, it would impugn his family name.

All of that should matter. But at the moment, his only true concern centered on losing Holly.

Will arrived in the drawing room last. He found Holly in an instant. Radiant in a scarlet gown, and with her hair hanging down in long, silvery-blond curls, with only the sides swept back, she glanced at him. Her expression remained particularly difficult to decipher. Perhaps his own jumbled emotions interfered with his perceptiveness.

He stumbled through dinner trying not to stare at Holly. His only consolation came from Holly's polite indifference to Lord Bradbury and his puzzled glances. At least the lord seemed to have no reason to believe Holly had a preference for him. Finally, Bradbury cast a thoughtful glance at Will and his eyes widened in understanding. A faintly wry twitch to his lips, and a raise of his glass toward Will, indicated he was stepping aside like a gentleman. Will gave up the last of his resentment toward the lord and silently wished him well.

After dessert, the ladies stood and left the room. Mrs. Gray never glanced his way. Mr. Gray leaned forward and quirked his brows at Will in a silent challenge. Did Holly tell him what Will had done? At last, Mr. Gray's mouth twitched in a faintly encouraging smile. Will still had one ally. He let out his breath.

Her gaze still enigmatic, Holly left the table last. At the doorway, she cast a glance over her shoulder at him. At the last second, her lips curved, just the tiniest bit.

His pathetically hopeful heart stood up and crowed. Maybe they had a chance after all. Or she had decided on a fitting way to seek revenge. No, that seemed out of character for her. Nevertheless, he deserved whatever she decided to mete out.

The conversation turned to hunting. Young Rudolph joined in, surprising the others with his knowledge of hunting dogs. When the topic changed to the uncommonly cold weather, he slumped. Poor lad would probably rather have livelier topics, or younger dinner companions.

Will glanced at the clock. Nerves and anticipation made him jumpy and impatient. After a respectable wait, and a few more glances at the clock, Will excused himself. For good or ill, he would face his future with the dignity of an Englishman.

Chapter Nineteen

Holly headed to the conservatory. Inside the room where it all began, she halted. Moonlight poured in through the windows and glittered on the snow outside. She moved deeper and deeper into the seating area amidst the indoor garden. Passing plants, flowers, small trees, and pieces of furniture, she moved through the room, blowing out lamps. At the lamp nearest the settee in a group of chairs next to the row of windows, she paused. No, she would leave this one on. No chance of mistake this time. She sat in the exact spot where her 'ghost' had kissed her.

She waited. Five minutes passed. Ten. What if he didn't come? What if he had decided that such a mopey and unforgiving child was not worth the trouble?

There! What was that? A faint rustle. She paused and held her breath.

"Who's there?" she whispered.

Had she imagined the sound? She raised her chin and wrapped her shawl more tightly around her to ward off the room's chill.

After glancing about the room, most of which

remained too dark to see beyond patches of moonlight on the floor, she turned to admire the snowy wonderland glittering beneath the cloudless night sky. It was every bit as lovely as it had been on that fateful night. The moon, no longer perfectly round, hung in the starry sky almost as bright as the night she half-believed she'd encountered a ghost.

"There you are," a low, male voice murmured.

She turned. Will stepped out of the shadows into the light. Nervous exhilaration filled her at the sight of his beloved face. He stood so stiffly, his expression so serious, so wary, that she hardly recognized him. Had all his feelings for her faded? Had she waited too long after seeing his message in the snow?

"Thank you for coming," she said. She patted the seat next to her. "I got your message in the snow."

Cautious and stiff, he approached, step by agonizing step. Something about him seemed different. His clothes rustled as he sat next to her. His warm scent invoked a sense of belonging, of home. She ached for his usual, lighthearted manner. Would the Will she'd grown to love ever return, or had she hurt him so deeply that he was lost to her?

She twisted her hands together. "I apologize for my ungracious reception to your confession this morning. I was overset and I fear I behaved rather badly."

"You were justified." So serious, almost grim, he studied her.

A crack opened up in her heart. She had done this. She had wounded him. She swallowed. "I took it too far. I was not only hurt and angry, but my pride got in the way. I'm sorry."

His dark eyes darted between hers. "Do you forgive me, then?"

She clasped her hands in front of her in a pleading gesture. "Of course I do. We all say or do things we later regret. Good people sometimes make bad choices."

The tension in his shoulders eased and his eyes lightened. Did that mean he still cared?

Timidly, she asked, "Do you forgive me for being so angry for so long?"

"There is nothing to forgive, love." Warmth and a tenderly soft light shone in his expression.

Love. Oh, how she adored hearing him call her that! "Can we start anew?"

"I don't think I can. But we could recreate the first time we met here, only do a proper job of it." That roguishness joined the tenderness in his expression.

Her nervous exhilaration split into a hundred lights. "I do believe that would be prudent. And enjoyable." She cocked her head, finally spotting what had seemed different about him. "You aren't wearing your spectacles."

A sheepish smile touched his mouth. "Well, they say it's wrong to hit a person wearing them, so I thought I'd save you the dilemma in case you were leaning that direction."

She laughed softly. "You didn't really think I'd slap you, did you?"

"Not really. But I wouldn't have blamed you. I do have another confession." A wry smile touched those lips she hoped would soon be pressing against hers.

"Oh dear," she said in a playfully sober voice. "Very well, I'll try to be more gracious about this one."

He leaned in closer. "I don't need to wear spectacles."

"No? Then why do you?"

"Everyone of my acquaintance who wears them is studious and sober. I thought if I wore them, I would adopt some of those traits."

She almost laughed out loud. "Did it help?"

"Not as well as I had hoped." He grinned unrepentantly. "I am glad. Otherwise, I might not have found you."

"So, sometimes the best thing to do is behave badly."

"Sometimes. Within reason."

"Are you about to behave badly now?"

245

"Oh yes," he groaned. Raw desire glimmered in his eyes. "You are so lovely in the moonlight."

He touched her cheek with a warm, gentle, ungloved hand, and leaned in. He pressed his lips to hers. Soft, tender, invigorating, his kiss immobilized her. Tingles raced through her, leaving sizzling trails. His lips moved across hers, an offering, a gift. As before, he tasted of citrus and cinnamon, exotic, and wholly pleasant. The heat of his lips created an answering warmth inside. Oh heavens, the sensation superseded all other kisses. With both hands, he cradled her face, all the while this exquisitely delicious sensation carried her closer to a height she longed to reach. That previously untouched place in her heart, the one only Will had found, awoke and sang. Every bone, muscle, and sinew in her body turned to liquid. Will kissed her over and over, deeper each time, while a now-familiar, sweet ache expanded. Each time, love and joy built inside her until thought fled and only sensation remained.

Holly sighed. Will's soft moan came in reply. The kiss ended. Soft kisses trailed along her cheek, her eyelids, her brow. Holly remained motionless, spellbound by the beauty and power and the wholeness of Will's kiss. She kept her eyes closed another heartbeat, unwilling to lose the triumphant joy encompassing her. She opened her eyes.

Still cradling her face, Will smiled. "I'm still here."

"That was even better," she murmured.

He grinned.

She touched his face. "Knowing it was you made all the difference."

He softly ran a hand over her hair. "You wore it down. For me?"

"You mentioned you wanted to see it down sometime. I thought it a fitting part of my apology."

"You didn't need to, but it's beautiful. Thank you. You are beautiful—in every way."

She gave him an arch look. "Do you have any more secrets?"

"Only one: I love you."

She might very well smile all the rest of her life, so full was her happiness. It seemed the Yule log did, indeed, bring good fortune; it brought them a wealth of love. "I love you, Will."

Delight and surprise lit his face. "Do you? Do you truly?"

"Yes, I do." Maybe she was gushing, but she didn't care.

"I will court you as long as you and your father desire, but I mean to marry you. Will you at least *consider* marrying me?"

Mrs. William Berry. Holly Berry. "Hmm."

247

Doubt touched his mouth. "You aren't sure you want to marry a vicar?"

"I'm not sure I want my name to be Holly Berry."

He blinked. Then laughed. She joined in and they laughed together.

"Holly Berry." He guffawed again. "Every time I say your name I will remember our first Christmas. And our first kisses."

"If you give me plenty more kisses, Sir Ghost, yes, I have every intention of marrying you, provided our courtship is long enough to satisfy my parents. Until my Papa gives his formal consent, ours must be a secret engagement."

He pretended to consider. "Another secret? Very well, your wish is my command, love. But first, another kiss?"

"Oh, please."

He proceeded to fulfill her request. No mistletoe nor ghosts invited.

Author's Notes:

Telling scary ghost stories is an age-old tradition dating so far back that I couldn't find its origin, but it reaches back at least as far as the 1500's.

Most of our familiar traditional Christmas Carols are relatively new and weren't around during the Regency. For this story, I did my best to choose song titles that had been written before 1813. However, it is possible not all of these carols I named had reached England from their native countries. I used some creative license for these loved carols.

The custom of walking to church instead of taking a carriage is based on an English law intended to allow the working class to rest on the Sabbath, including coach drivers.

Travel in winter in England during the Regency was extremely hazardous and therefore rarely done. Christmas house parties any distance away were more feasible after the arrival of railroads which happened after 1840. Of course, I and every other author I have read, largely ignores this, although it is the reason my hero cannot go home for Christmas and why his sister Mary and her family arrive so late.

The Twelve Days of Christmas started on Dec. 26th, which was Boxing Day, and ended on January 6th. Christmas Day was not generally much more than a church holy day among the upper classes, although customs did vary from place to place and family to family. I, of course, exercised my creative license and had the local tradition include many Old Christmas customs of the season for the purpose of making this novel more fun for my beloved readers. And besides, some noble families really did have these wonderful customs, even in the Regency, so it wasn't too big a stretch.

About the Author

Best-selling author, Donna Hatch, is a hopeless romantic and adventurer at heart, the force that drove her to write and publish twenty historical romance titles, including the award-winning "Rogue Hearts Series." She is a multi-award winner, a sought-after workshop presenter, and juggles multiple volunteer positions as well as her six (yes, that is 6) children. A music lover, Donna sings and plays the harp, and loves to ballroom dance. Donna and her family recently transplanted from her native Arizona to the Pacific Northwest where she and her husband of over twenty years are living proof that there really is a happily ever after.

Dear Reader,

Sign up for Donna Hatch's newsletter and receive a free e-book! To subscribe and get a free eBook of her full-length Regency Romance novel, The Stranger She Married, download here:

http://donnahatch.com/stranger-she-married-free-download/

Your email will not be shared, and you may unsubscribe at any time.

Reviews are appreciated, but there is no obligation.

If you lipke this story, please help spread the word and rate or review it on Amazon here: https://www.amazon.com/dp/B076B6Z7GZ

Please also consider reviewing *Christmas Secrets* on Goodreads and other book review sites.

To find out more about this author and her books, visit

Website at www.donnahatch.com

Blog: www.donnahatch.com/blog Connect on Facebook: www.facebook.com/RomanceAuthorDonnaHatch

Follow on Twitter: https://twitter.com/donnahatch

Thank you!

64107790R00146

Made in the USA
San Bernardino, CA
20 December 2017